Slippers & Chains
Second Base

Raven ShadowHawk

little
vamppress

Slippers & Chains:
Second Base

Published in November 2015 by Little Vamp Press

Cover design: 'ravenink'
Editor: Leah Osbourne

ISBN: 978-0-9933446-1-9
First Edition

ACKNOWLEDGEMENTS

A lovely collection of beta readers must be mentioned this time around, as your help has been fantastic. Very many thanks to Summer Ross, Shelli Rosewarne and Noelle Riches.

I'd also like to tip my hat to 'ravenink' who continues to do fantastic cover work with the briefs I spit at stupid hours of the night.

DEDICATION

To my Funk Master

KAREN

Karen breathed deep and sank deeper into the embrace of the ropes. Soft cords bit the skin on her arms and set it tingling. 'Does it have to be that tight?'

'Yes, it does.' Shirtless, Dan stood to her right, his eyes bright in the dim light. The fine dusting of hair across his chest formed a trail that teased along his belly before vanishing into the low slung waist of his trousers. Sweat glistened on his forehead and shoulders in tear-drop sparkles.

God, he's hot.

'But—' A low buzz caught her attention. The egg. She almost forgot. The wet hum of it made muscles low in her body clench. The dull vibration made everything else ache. Even her teeth.

'Do you want to fall out?'

A ripple of fear thrilled through her body. 'No . . .'

'Then relax and enjoy it. I've watched the videos; I know what I'm doing.'

Though he spoke with quiet, easy confidence, Karen couldn't help but whisper a small prayer. Videos on YouTube, filmed and executed by professionals differed greatly to an impromptu bondage session in their living room. Even with proper hooks, knots and ropes. She eyed the thick, metal hook screwed into the ceiling, supported by a wide base. 'What did it say about blood supply?'

Dan laughed. 'Stop worrying. You won't be up there much longer. I just want to spank you a bit.' He stroked her rear, teasing the edge of her lacy red knickers. The other hand flicked at the crystal weights dangling from the clamps on her sore, puffy nipples. 'And maybe, if you're good, I'll use the wand again.'

Karen bit her lip. She fucking loved that wand. The smell of ozone still hung in the air and her back prickled at the memory of fizzing sparks dancing over her skin.

'Do it. Please.'

'Have you earned it? Done everything I told you?'

A burst of copper-sweetness flooded Karen's tongue. She'd bitten too hard. 'Yes.'

'Have you?' Dan's voice roughened. Gruff. His eyes narrowed as he leaned close, tossing his head to flick a curl hair from his eyes. 'I don't think so, little miss. You couldn't even finish a decent blow job.'

'That's not my fault.' Karen kicked out with both legs. The ropes binding her prevented more than inadequate flailing an inch in either direction, but her shifting weight swung her body in a small circle. She moaned, relaxed into the ropes and watched the floor spin beneath her. 'Please Sir, that wasn't my fault. You teased me.'

'So?'

'With a vibrator. How can I concentrate when you push that thing into me?'

Dan licked his lips and gave a feral grin. 'I don't remember pushing anything into you.'

Another moan. Karen's skin tingled with the memory.

Kneeling on a cushion with hands and arms bound, a ball gag pressed against her teeth, Karen watched as Hannah appeared beneath her. Naked but for a tiny thong, the curvy, curly haired woman raised a long wand with a vibrating head and shoved it against Karen's screaming pussy. The thrill of it, the delicious pressure against her sensitive clit made her come on the spot, even with her mouth full of Dan's solid, pulsing cock.

Back in the present moment, Dan swatted her backside, sending her spinning in a fast, tight circle. 'God, I love this thing. You look great in it.'

'The wand?' A hopeful lilt lifted her voice.

'Fine. Just once more.' He stepped back, retrieving the long black stem from the sofa. When he fitted the glass rod and switched it on, a loud crackle filled the air.

Karen tensed. *This is it. Here we go.*

She watched Dan, wary of the wand. Part of her longed to linger on his face but the rest couldn't bear to be unprepared when the rounded glass nub neared her skin.

Tiny hairs on the back of her neck stood to attention. A shudder rippled through her bound body, shoulders to toes, then back up again. She clenched her fists. 'Oh, God . . .'

Dan stroked the air near her shoulder with the end of the wand. Her skin prickled. The wand crackled. From the corner of her eye, Karen glimpsed a jagged spike of purple light flash between the glass and her skin. The stinging sensation struck her shoulder and spiralled outward.

She yelped. 'Wait a minute.'

His hand froze. 'What?'

Words caught in the back of her throat. She fought to form a coherent sentence. 'The egg. Each time you prick me, you turn up the egg, you promised.'

Smug knowing filled Dan's eyes. 'So *that's* why you want it.' He switched off the wand. The crackling died away. Silence filled the room, broken only by Karen's harried breathing.

'No, no, no,' she whined, jerking against the ropes. 'You haven't let me come yet. Please?'

'You don't need an egg for that.'

Dropping to his knees, Dan reached up between her bound legs and dipped his fingers into her hot slit. He wriggled them around. Karen whined and thrashed against the ropes. The harsh bite of the knots chaffed her skin while both weighted nipple clamps swung to and fro. When he flicked, Karen couldn't hold back a shriek.

'Please, please, please.'

His fingers pushed further, finally touching the vibrating egg pushed deep into her moist centre. 'Not yet. I'm considering leaving this here.'

'God, no. You can't.' Desperation gave her voice a shrill edge. The thought of having to endure an entire evening of intermittent stimulation made her half mad with the desire to come. Especially when she considered the plans for the rest of the evening.

'My mum,' she whispered. '*Your* mum . . .'

'What about them?' Dan flicked the weighted clamps one last time before pulling a tiny remote from his pocket. He pressed a button near the top.

The egg's rhythm intensified inside Karen's body, an incredible pace that thrummed inside her with such intensity that white spots danced before her eyes. She tried to draw her legs together, but the knot work prevented even that small mercy. Her fingers twitched. Toes curled. The wet squelch of her overexcited pussy soon drowned out the buzz.

'Fuck,' she murmured. 'Fuck, fuck, fuck.'

Dan's hand twitched and the egg reached its most intense setting. Karen spluttered and squirmed in her bonds as his hands stroked and pinched her body. At irregular intervals he paused to flick the crystal weights. Mostly he stroked every inch of her exposed skin.

'Come for me, Kaz.'

Karen jerked in the ropes, then let herself go, clenching her teeth to hold back the scream. Wave after delicious wave of ecstasy flooded her body and the egg wedged inside her gave a moist burble before bursting free of her spasming pussy. It hit the floor and buzzed across the carpet.

The sensations faded slowly.

She opened her eyes far enough to see Dan crouched nearby, watching her through hooded eyes. 'You have no idea how sexy you look when you do that.'

Karen licked her lips. She wanted to speak but the words wouldn't come. Instead she nodded and relaxed fully into the ropes. The shift in tension made her swing back and forth, a naked, gasping pendulum in the middle of the room.

Warm pleasure filled her stomach. Not the skin-tingling, lust-firing sort of pleasure. Softer. Gentle. Rooted in the loving expression of Dan's eyes and the softness of his voice. Her Dom melted away to leave Dan himself; the man who loved her. The man she loved back more than she ever thought possible.

While her body drifted back from its physical high, her mind took a spiralling journey of its own.

His gaze settled on her face and she drank in his features. The dark shadow of stubble flecked with grey. Crooked nose. Dimpled chin. 'You're incredible,' she whispered.

He lowered his head until a familiar curl of hair flopped down and hid his eyes. 'No more than you.'

'Kiss me.'

He cupped her cheek, steadying her long enough to feed his tongue into her mouth. She sucked on it, kissing deep and long until her over excited groin stirred to request an encore.

'I love you,' she whispered.

'Right back at you, Kaz. And I'm sorry.'

She blinked. 'For what?'

The answer came as an explosion of pain from her left nipple. Dan loosened the clamp and pulled them away, allowing blood to rush back into the sensitive nub. Karen shrieked and thrashed. Nonsensical babble fell from her lips as the raging pain crested a peak and became pleasure. The right nipple roared to join the first. Her sudden orgasm crashed in and left stars dancing across her eyes.

Dan's tongue lapped against the soreness, hot moisture flicking over and over. It hurt. God, it hurt. But it hurt so good.

She moaned and shuddered through the little after-shocks while he teased her with his tongue.

'Fuck me,' she breathed.

'Are you sure? Aren't you tired?' Dan gripped his cock through the front of his trousers and gave a crooked smile. 'I was saving this for later, but if you really can't wait . . .'

'No, no, please, I need a break.'

'Sure.' He grabbed a bean bag from the other side of the room and shoved it beneath her. Only then did he winch her down via the rope looped into the ceiling.

The leather surface kissed her sensitive skin and brought another moan from her lips. But the ropes around her thighs, arms and stomach allowed her no more than a wiggle.

Eventually, Dan untied her, jerking on the loops in each knot to release her limbs in stages. Back first, her spine straightening as ropes slithered free. Then elbows. Ankles. Thighs. Knees. Wrists.

Karen listened to Dan's soft humming as he worked to undo all the fascinating knot work. Conscious control returned to each body part in turn. She likened it to emerging from deep, restful sleep.

When her arms jerked, then slumped, Karen eased them round to a more natural position. Thick rope marks lined her biceps and wrists, a faint redness that she treasured. Then the ropes about her thighs flexed and fell loose.

She grinned and stretched out across the bean bag.

Dan appeared in her field of vision. 'You okay?'

She pulled him down on to her for another lingering kiss. 'I'm great. Thank you. I'm good until tomorrow.'

'We can't play with her straight away, you know. She might not show up.'

'I can hope, can't I?' Karen grinned. 'Maybe she'll arrive with a friend and we'll all get on so well that we can't help but fall into bed.'

Dan gave an appreciative 'mmm' sound. 'Three lovely subs. All for me. That *would* be something.'

'Or one for me,' she ventured, still lost in the fantasy. 'A sub under me. And I could sit on his face while this new girl deep throats him.'

He shook his head. 'You could sit on *her* face while the other goes down on *her*. That sounds much more like it.'

'Come on,' she teased. 'You wouldn't like seeing me flog a guy? You could watch. Remember how you got after Sugar Dust? Nothing like a kink club to bring out new ideas. I could be 'Bitch Queen' again.'

'Ha,' he pressed a tender kiss to her lips. 'Tease. What do you want another guy for? You've got me.'

'So I get to flog you?' Though she fought it, her voice emerged dry and sharp.

'Not bloody likely.' Another kiss, then he pulled away. 'So, was that enough? I figured four orgasms would probably relax you but six seemed a safer bet.'

Hiding her disappointment beneath a smile, Karen nodded. 'Yes, I feel better.' She studied his face. Bit her lip.

Was *now* the moment to ask about subs again? Before he drifted too far from the pleasurable place they both occupied while playing.

The door bell rang.

Dan stroked her jaw with the tip of his finger. 'I'd better get that.' He stood, and the moment was lost.

She sighed. 'Guess I'll clear up.' She glanced at the collection of toys strewn across the rug.

He slid off her body and left. The ache of his departure was a physical thing. A yearning in her skin that tightened her chest.

I'm addicted to him. I really am.

Faint, Karen heard the front door open and close, followed by the rumble of low voices.

She tugged a dressing gown over her nakedness and put the toys, one by one, into the large pine chest beside the bookcase. She *would* clean them—that was her job—but later. The rope she coiled into neat loops and placed alongside the toys with the weighted nipple clamps and silenced vibrating egg.

A moment later Dan opened the door and peered through. 'It's only Pete.'

Oh. Great.

A prickle of unease rolled down the back of her neck. 'Will you guys want a beer?'

Dan grinned, oblivious to her discomfort. 'Sure, thanks.' He slipped out of sight again.

Karen cinched the dressing gown around her waist. The hem brushed her knees, a modest length, but not enough.

I've got to change before he sees me. Especially if they're drinking.

Tiptoeing from the room, she paused at the closed door to the study and listened to the low burble of voices within.

She shook her head, clutched the neck of her gown closed and darted up the stairs.

DAN

Dan slouched against the wall, watching his friend pull four-packs from a plastic bag. 'She won't be back again,' he picked up where he'd left off. 'Says she has a new Dom and that he doesn't want her playing away from him. Fair enough. I wouldn't want Karen playing with anyone else.'

Glass clinked and packets rustled as Pete piled them on the table. When the bag was empty he crunched it up and tossed it into a corner. 'So you need a new girl?'

'I don't know. I want one, but Karen is still . . . you know? She likes sharing, but prefers one on one time.'

'Who doesn't?'

He looked away. 'So tomorrow, we're meeting a new potential at the munch.'

'Potential,' Pete scoffed. 'You make it sound like an interview.'

'It is in a way. We meet this girl, decide if we like her and give her a trial run. If she fits in with us, she joins the Library. If not, we don't see her again.'

'I still don't get how it works. Women aren't just books you can check in and out when you want.'

'Actually, that's exactly how it works.'

'And Karen is what? Head Librarian?'

Dan shoved off the wall. He snatched beers from the table and slotted the bottles into a bucket filled with ice. 'Why does it bother you so much?'

Pete's expression hardened, all twisted lip and narrow eyes. 'You don't seem to realise how lucky you are. Why do you need other women, when you have Karen willing to do whatever you want? *When*ever you want? Don't think I didn't see you last night. She had her foot in your trousers.'

'It was under the table.'

'We were at Pizza Express! There were kids there.'

Dan added a few soft drinks to the bucket. 'Nobody saw. Stop worrying.'

'I'm not worrying.'

'Stop being jealous then.'

'Jealous? Screw you.'

'Ha, you wish.'

'I'm just—never mind. I'll get the rest of the bags.' Pete stalked out, grumbling under his breath.

When sure he was alone, Dan took a moment to huff a curl of hair out of his eyes. Though he longed to pace, the dozens of bags dotting the floor left him with too little room. Instead he chewed the inside of his cheek, glaring at the beer.

It's none of his business. This is about me and Karen. Why does he even care?

The doorbell rang again. He stomped back to the door and jerked it open.

A short woman with straight brown hair and a solemn expression, flinched back from him. 'What's up with you?'

'Sam?' He stepped back to let her through. 'Nothing. I'm fine.'

'Of course you are.'

He swallowed the sharp response rising in his throat. 'Where's Cindy?'

'Parking. Why is your street so packed? It's a nightmare.'

Dan narrowed his eyes. 'Have you been speaking to my mother?'

'No, why?'

'Nothing. Just come in, will you? Grab a beer or something.'

Sam shook her head. 'I'm on call, but I'll have some lemonade if you have any.'

'Check the ice bucket.'

As she walked through, Pete hurried up the path carrying two plastic bags. He shivered as he approached. 'You didn't tell me she was coming.'

Dan eyed his harried expression. 'Didn't think I had to. She's with Cindy, I figured it was a given.'

'I thought they broke up.'

'They did. Then made up. Then broke up. Then made up. You know what it's like with those two.'

'Yes but—this is bad.' His fingers twitched on the handles to the carrier bags.

'What have you done?'

'Nothing.'

'Pete . . .'

He gazed at the floor, watching his shuffling feet. 'I've got weed in my pocket.'

Dan rolled his eyes. 'So leave it in the car.'

'This neighbourhood? It'll get robbed quicker than chocolate at Slimming World.'

He turned back towards the hallway. 'Then bring it in. Whatever, I don't care. Just come inside.'

'Dan, she's a policewoman.'

Impatience gave his voice a rough edge. 'And her girlfriend is the biggest pothead I've ever met. I'm sure she has other things to deal with besides you and a bit of weed.'

Still Pete lingered. 'It's not just in my pocket.'

Dan sucked in a deep breath then let it out slow. 'Tell me.'

'My cousin made biscuits. I couldn't eat them all so I brought them.'

Dan's heart gave a little flutter. 'You brought hash-cakes to my house warming party? My parents are going to be here.'

Pete looked nervously into the house. 'Keep your voice down.'

'Jesus, Pete, are you crazy? Isn't this going to be hard enough?'

'I thought you'd want some. You used to.'

'And I *used* to jerk off to anime but I don't do that any more either. Mum will be here in half an hour. Where are they?'

Pete gave a slow blink.

'The biscuits!'

'In the kitchen.'

Dan dashed back into the house. In the kitchen, he caught his foot on a bag of snacks and stumbled into the counter. He caught himself with his hands. 'Ow . . .' Pain speared through his locked elbows.

A shadow fell over him. Sam extended one hand. 'Take it easy, Bolt. You okay?'

He stood, awkward and stiff as his knees joined the song of pain. 'I'm fine.'

'Still don't believe you, Dan.' She took a huge bite of the biscuit in her other hand. Crumbs rained down her chin. 'Do you need help in here? I don't mind.'

Dan looked at the biscuit. Small. Dark. Studded with chocolate chips. 'Where did you get that?'

She hooked a thumb at a large plastic box beside the kettle. Open and stuffed with cookies.

Fuck.

'They're great.' She gestured with the remaining crescent before ramming it into her mouth. 'Karen make them?' More crumbs flew.

He froze, looking at Sam, the box, then back again. 'Oh, God, Sam.'

'I know, they're for the party, but I'm starving. I only had a few.'

'A few?' he squeaked. A giant, invisible fist squeezed the air from his lungs.

'Okay, three, but they're really good.'

'Sam.' He buried his face in his hands. 'Jesus, Sam.'

'What? Cindy's right; you *are* high strung. They're just cookies. You've got loads.' She snagged another and ate half in one smooth movement.

'Sam those cookies have got—'

'Samantha!' Pete barrelled into the room, dumped his bags on the dining table and rushed over to gather Sam into a bone crunching hug. He plucked the cookie from her fingers. 'How the hell are you?'

'Um . . .' She struggled, feet waving three inches off the ground. 'Good, I suppose.'

'And Cindy?'

'Parking the car. Put me down.'

'What?' Pete frowned.

Sam glared. 'Put me down and give me my cookie.'

Dan shook his head as his friend lowered Sam to the floor.

This ought to be good.

'Thanks.' She brushed herself off. 'My cookie?'

Pete stared at the half eaten snack as though he had no idea what it was. 'I—no. Sorry. Haven't tried one yet and they look really good.'

'There's a whole tub right here.'

Pete crammed the cookie crescent into his mouth and grabbed the box. 'I'll take these.'

Dan snorted. He couldn't help it. 'The damage is done. Put them down, Pete.'

'What damage?' Sam held up her hands. 'I only had a few. Are they really *that* special?'

This time he couldn't hold the laughter in. 'You could say that.'

'They're just chocolate chip.' She brushed crumbs off her blouse.

'You didn't taste anything else?'

'Maybe a bit of a weird aftertaste, but that's nothing to—' She broke off. Her eyes widened. 'What have you done?'

'Me?' Dan touched his chest. 'Nothing. Ask my idiot friend over there.'

Pete shot him a 'thanks mate' glare before turning to face Sam. 'I can explain.'

'What's wrong with those cookies?'

'Nothing,' he stammered.

'Funny, but I don't believe you. You and Dan are terrible liars.'

Cindy breezed into the kitchen. She wore tight black trousers slung low on the hips and a fishnet shirt over a shocking-pink bra, a strong contrast to Sam's modest blouse and knee length skirt. 'Hey bitches. Ooo, cookies!' She reached around Pete and snagged one. 'I love chocolate chip. Home made?' She bit. Chewed. Swallowed. Grinned. 'Fuck me, that's strong shit. Who are you trying to kill?'

Sam folded her arms. 'Will someone tell me what's in those cookies?'

Pete groaned. 'My cousin made them. I didn't—'

'Well, tell your cousin she's a fucking genius.' Cindy demolished the rest of the biscuit.

'His name is Mark.'

'Bullshit.' She reached for another and examined it. 'No man can cook up space-cookies this good. This has to be a *woman's* work.'

Sam slumped against the sideboard. 'Space-cookies? Like hash? As in weed?'

Dan watched the understanding dawn on her face and took a giant step back. *Here we go . . .*

Pete slammed the lid into place. Wet his lips. 'I'm sorry, okay? I didn't know you were going to come in here and stuff your face. Who does that anyway? Who just walks into someone's house and eats their food?'

'It's a party!' Sam snarled. 'Of course I ate the food. Do you have any idea how long that stuff stays in your system? I'm on call. I have a shift tomorrow.'

Cindy cocked her head. The long tail of her ice-white hair flicked over one shoulder. 'Wait, you ate one? Why? When did you get all loose and free?'

'I didn't know.'

'How many?'

Sam glared at the floor. 'Six.'

Dan frowned. 'Blimey, did you inhale them? You told me three.'

'I lied,' she snapped. 'Am I the only one not allowed to lie?'

Cindy slapped her thigh. 'Oh my fucking god, you're going to be so high.'

'This isn't funny!'

'It is. You get so horny when you're high; why do you think I keep offering to cook?'

'You cook because it's your turn.' Sam frowned, tugging on a lock of her hair.

Dan inched away from the two women. He saw the storm brewing and preferred to be out of range.

Cindy winked. 'I cook because I get to spice up the food.'

'You spike my food?' Sam's voice rose several octaves.

Cindy closed the small space between them and tucked that maltreated wisp of straight, brown hair behind Sam's ear. 'You're so fucking hot when you're pissed at me. That's the other reason. I love it when you go all *copper*.' Still smiling, Cindy shoved her girlfriend against the sideboard. 'We're gonna have so much fun tonight. You'll be high, I'll be drunk and we'll fuck like bunnies until we're too sore to move.'

Pete's mouth dropped open.

'You don't want to see that.' Dan grabbed his friend by the arm and hauled him into the living room.

'Don't I?' Pete cast wistful glances over his shoulder. 'They're real, proper lesbians, aren't they?'

'Cindy is. Sam's a bit more flexible.'

Pete licked his lips. 'How flexible?'

'Don't you dare, you horny bastard. And give me those cookies.' He snatched the box and put it on a bookcase. 'Leave her alone. Don't go near her. Don't touch her. Don't even talk to her.'

'But—'

Dan threw him a level look. 'When she gets off that high how do you think she'll feel? Trust me, leave her alone.'

Karen entered the living room.

Familiar warmth fanned across Dan's chest and groin when he saw her. His gaze traced the line of her jaw, the swell of her breasts and the incredible curve from her waist to her hips. So beautiful. Even more in the tight jeans she wore, topped by a flowing, sleeveless shirt with a pattern of red and purple flowers. Purple always looked amazing against her skin.

A flash of light brought his attention to her wrist. His throat tightened. 'You're wearing the slave band.'

She nodded shyly, playing with the silver links. 'Is that okay? I know your mum will be here but it's important to me.'

Dan rushed forward and cut her off with a kiss. She melted into his embrace, soft and supple as a cat. Despite her recent orgasms she pressed against him, hot, needy, willing. Always willing. He slipped his hand beneath her shirt, stroking her ribs. At her bra, he thumbed her nipples through the cups until they stiffened. 'It's important to me too.'

'Thank you, Sir.'

He could think of nothing better than his submissive wearing their personal interpretation of a collar during their housewarming celebrations. For all his friends and family to see that she belonged to him, even if they didn't understand what the piece of jewellery really meant. Perfect.

Pete cleared his throat.

When Dan escaped the hypnotic pull of Karen's eyes, he found his friend studying the bookcase. 'Sorry.' As the word left his mouth he wanted it back. Why did he feel the need to apologise for a gesture of affection? In his own home?

Karen noticed Pete at the same moment and jerked away. She pressed her back to the door frame and smoothed her shirt over her stomach. 'Hey, Pete. How are you?'

'Fine,' he stared at the books.

Dan frowned. He imagined a thick wall of ice, with Karen and Pete on either side, talking across the awkward distance. 'What's wrong with you two?'

Pete shrugged.

Karen gazed at her toes.

He sighed. 'Is this about the cage? Still? Guys, I'm sorry but we've got to move on. It wasn't that big a deal, right?'

Discomfort centred on the memory forced him to lock the experience away in a far corner of his mind. Having to leave Karen in a three–by–three play cage was bad enough, but being forced to call Pete to rescue her was far worse.

Pete gave a tight smile. 'What are you talking about? I'm fine, mate. I've already forgotten everything I saw. We're good, right Kaz?'

Her smile didn't quite reach her eyes. 'We're good.'

Bullshit.

He longed to shake both of them. To grab their shoulders and jerk them back and forth until the lies ran clear. If only it were so simple.

With Karen, maybe—they were much better at talking since the trip to Sugar Dust—but Peter? The man clammed up tighter than an oyster when he wanted and nothing short of torture would open his mouth.

I don't have time for this.

'Fine. Whatever. I need a tablecloth.' He struck off for the kitchen.

Karen grabbed his arm. 'Don't go in there just yet.'

A keening groan floated through the closed door across the hallway.

Karen shrugged. 'I stopped to grab a beer and found Cindy with her head under Sam's skirt. If we don't disturb them they'll get it out of their system a lot faster.'

'I doubt that.' Dan rolled his eyes. 'Fucking lesbians.'

'Hey,' she slapped his arm. 'As if we haven't done worse. Remember last night?'

Dan did indeed recall; the damp cotton of Karen's underwear in his pocket and the delicious pressure of her toes as she massaged his cock beneath the table while he struggled to eat spaghetti carbonara. He remembered the delirious pleasure as he fumbled the remote in his pocket, occasionally giving the egg clamped inside her pussy a burst of high speed.

It was enough to make his cock twitch.

He shook his head. 'I'll not forget in a hurry. Believe me.'

Another loud moan came from the kitchen. Maniacal laughter. Something heavy thudded on to the floor. Shrieks of pleasure.

Dan turned back to the living room. 'Maybe we should get the sound system ready.'

Karen patted his arm. 'Good idea.'

KAREN

Karen refilled a bowl of nuts while swaying her hips to the pounding music.

The press of bodies, loud chatter and music collided to make thinking difficult. Not that it mattered. People seemed more concerned with dancing, eating and drinking.

She checked her phone, scrolling through her recent calls. Nothing yet. Not even a text message.

Maybe the train's late. Or she's stuck without a signal. She'd call if she could.

Her palms prickled with sweat. Karen wiped them on her jeans. To occupy her hands, she fussed with the links of her slave band, turning the rings back and forth on her slender fingers.

Three silver rings, attached to a bracelet by thin chains studded with white crystals like flakes of diamond.

Seeing it soothed her. Reminded her of the love shared between herself and Dan, hot, honest and deep.

She faced the room, smiling each time someone caught her eye. Colleagues from the university, various social workers from Dan's professional circle, the occasional closer friend. So many people turned out to wish herself and Dan well in their new home.

From the corner of her eye, she saw Dan fiddling with the stereo. As he stooped, the muscles across his back and shoulder bunched, released and bunched again. His hair curled over the back of his neck and shoulders.

He needs a trim.

She imagined doing it herself, running her fingers through the silky-soft strands to reveal the nape of his neck. She longed to kiss him. Or bite him.

Living with Dan was a dream come true. Waking to his face every morning, listening to his steady breathing every night. Washing his holey, mismatched socks, cooking his food, sharing his bath. She treasured every part of it.

A voice came from her right. 'Karen, I don't like the carpets.' Sharp. Slightly nasal. An inflection that spoke of dirty, smelly things in need of a wash.

She fixed a wide smile in place and turned to face her mother-in-law. 'Good evening, Maxine.'

The older woman wrinkled her surgically straightened nose. 'Haven't we already done all that?'

'You said hello to Dan, not me.'

'Oh, you silly thing.' Maxine waved her hand, a clatter of gold bracelets. 'It's implied. Hello Daniel and his darling significant other?'

Sarcastic bitch.

Karen struggled to moderate her tone. 'What's wrong with the carpets?'

'They're brown.'

'Egg-shell.'

'It looks dirty. Like some big, wet dog rolled all over it. Is it new?'

'Of course it is. What are you trying to say?'

Maxine glanced at her feet then up again, as if to leave her gaze on the carpet would render her dirty too. 'You never can tell. I hope you went to a proper store and not one of those cheap Asian places. It doesn't even match this gorgeous wallpaper.'

Karen grinned, a childish surge of triumph. 'You'll have to ask Dan: *he* chose the carpet. I bought the wallpaper.' She shoved passed Maxine before anything less delicate could pass her mouth. She angled herself toward Cindy, chatting gaily with Julian on the long sofa.

The older man stood when she approached. He held out his hands and she gladly clasped them in her own, leaning in to kiss his whiskery cheek. 'Hey.'

'Good evening, my dear. What a wonderful party. Thank you for inviting us.'

'Having fun?'

'Yes and having a splendid chat with your lovely friend. She's quite the charmer.'

Cindy gave a surprised bark of laughter. 'Steady on, grandpa.'

Karen smiled. For all her friend's unconventional appearance, Cindy always did have a way with words and a strong, magnetic charisma. 'Just don't let her draw you into politics. She's much less charming then.'

Cindy stuck up her middle finger, then fiddled with her white hair. 'Just because I have views, Kaz. You're so busy bending over for Wonder-Dan over there, you never think about the bigger picture. You two are pioneers. You should be thinking about what you can do for the world.'

'Pioneers?' If Cindy's crude language bothered Julian, he did a good job of keeping it to himself. Instead he returned to his seat and folded his hands in his lap. 'I know my son is a good man, but where does this pioneer talk come from?'

Karen opened her mouth, but Cindy got there first. 'Don't worry about it, Mr Scotney. I'm just playing.'

'Well, if we're that comfortable with each other, you'd better call me Julian.'

Karen skimmed the sofa. 'Where's Sam?'

A soft chuckle from Cindy. 'In the downstairs bathroom. She started to see colours so I told her to stay there for a bit.'

'How many of those stupid things did she eat?'

'She says six, but she's a shitty liar for a copper. More like ten. She'll be a mess. A dopey, giggling, horny mess.'

'Maybe I should check on her.'

'No, I'll go.' Cindy stood, brushed crumbs off her lap and marched away.

Julian thumbed his bristly upper lip. 'This is a lovely house, my dear. I'm glad to see you happy.'

She gazed at the links of the slave band draped over her wrist. 'I've never been happier.'

'Daniel is happy too, I hope you know that. *You* make him happy.'

Karen squirmed and rubbed the back of her neck. She plucked a sausage roll from the stack on the table and popped it into her mouth.

'I've embarrassed you. I just . . .' He looked up as he sought the words he wanted. His gaze fell on the bracket beside the lampshade, remnants of Dan's suspension play. 'What's that?'

'Nothing. And I'm not embarrassed, just—' she fished around for an appropriate diversion and saw Maxine running a finger along the top of the TV. 'Your wife doesn't seem to agree.'

Julian cleared his throat hard enough to make his whiskers billow in the draught. 'My wife hides pleasure well, that's certain, but she's happy too. Trust me. Daniel means more to her than anything and even she sees that you're good for him. Try not to take anything she says too personally.'

Karen didn't speak. Her fingers opened and closed over her palms, tight fists she had to shake away. 'She hates me.'

'No, no, she doesn't. Don't believe that for a moment. It's just hard to lose her baby boy.'

'Dan is a grown man. He doesn't even wet the bed any more.'

Julian stared, his eyes wide with alarm. An instant later he chuckled, puffing through his beard like Santa Claus. '*That* is why he likes you. You're fiery. Funny. Cruel, sometimes, with that sharp tongue of yours. But I mean it, no mother ever truly believes their son has grown up. Maybe one day you'll understand.' He gave her stomach a meaningful glance.

'Me?' Her voice emerged high and squeaky, a cassette tape played too fast. 'What?' Karen took a step back. Gripped her stomach. A moment later she released her grip as though stunned by the reflex. Damp palms. Again. She wiped them on her jeans. 'No, no, we don't want—I mean, we never planned—'

His smile drooped a little. 'Oh.'

'Not that I wouldn't—*we* wouldn't. I just—we—'

Her pocket began to vibrate.

Thank God.

Groping for the mobile, Karen gave Julian an apologetic glance and backed away. 'Sorry. I need to take this.' She left him in the middle of the laughing, drinking crowd and tried to steady the race of her heart.

Fuck. Where did that *come from?*

She answered the phone. 'Hello?'

'Hey, sweetie, it's me. What number are you, again?'

Karen tightened her grip on the phone. 'Mama?'

'Is it number three or seven? I can hear music but I'm not sure which house it's coming from.'

'We're seven.'

'Good. Come answer the door.'

Eyes closed, Karen slipped the phone into her pocket. A moment later, a soft hand settled on her shoulder. Julian stood at her side, his bushy eyebrows drawn down in concern.

'Are you okay?'

'Fine I—my mum is here.'

His eyes brightened. 'Wonderful. It will be nice to finally meet her. Your father too?'

Karen stiffened. 'No.' Breaking away, she shoved her way through the crowds to the front door. A large shadow loomed against the textured glass.

She took a deep breath. Opened the door.

Charlaine Owusu blew through like a whirlwind, planting loud, wet kisses against Karen's cheek. 'Hey, sweetie, this is a lovely house. You've done so well.' She brandished a huge box wrapped in silver paper.

'Hi, Mama. Thanks.' Karen wiped a smear of lipstick off her cheek and took the gift. 'How are you?' She took in the tiny wrinkles at the corners of her mother's eyes, the familiar beauty spot on her right cheek. Short hair with subtle hints of white. A tiny gold crucifix winked against her collar bone. Gold crosses dangled from her pierced ears.

'Wonderful. Excellent. Peaceful.' She paused in the doorway and beckoned. 'We both are.'

'Both? You brought a date?'

'Yes. Is that okay?'

'Of course it is! I've been hoping you would ditch that creep—' Karen broke off when she saw her mother's expression. 'You didn't ditch him, did you?'

'Karen—'

Her grip tightened on the box. 'I told you not to bring him to my house.'

'I thought you would . . .' Charlaine's shoulders drooped.

'What? Change my mind? No, Mama, I don't want him in my house.'

'But we've come all this way.'

Karen dropped the box. Something inside shattered. 'I don't care. He's not welcome.'

A shadow fell over them. Karen flinched back, crushing the box with her heel. She looked up, then up some more. Saw white teeth with a flash of gold in one corner. Thick, jowly cheeks, narrow eyes and a hat with a wide brim that cast a shadow over the rest of the face.

'Robert,' she snarled.

The man stepped forward. 'Don't call mi that.'

'I've got a bunch of other names, if you prefer.'

'I'm your father.'

'No, you're not.' Karen struck the wall with her palm. Even from a distance his breath reeked of rum. 'And you're *not* welcome here.'

He snorted. 'So who's going to keep mi out? You? This lanky white man you decided to shack up with?'

'Please, don't.' Charlaine touched his arm. He shook her off.

'Shut up, woman. You brought mi here, now I'm sure as hell staying for a bite to eat. And a drink. Get inside or out mi way, because I'm going in.'

Karen watched her mother hesitate. Indecision shone behind those big, dark eyes. Then she shook her head and stepped back. Robert shoved through and straight toward the sound of voices, kicking the silver box aside on the way.

Karen shook her head. 'Why, Mama?'

'I need him.'

She wanted to scream. Hot fury knotted her stomach and made her head throb. 'You don't.'

'Oh, sweetie, I do. I really do.'

Karen's anger seeped away, replaced by the chill of confusion and worry. The woman cringing in the doorway looked so unlike her mother. Charlaine Owusu was a bright, outspoken, healthy-looking woman. As Karen looked harder, she saw dark circles beneath her mother's eyes and a sag to the skin around her neck that never used to be there. Even her trembling fingers were thinner than she remembered, the gold wedding ring on her left hand held in place with little lumps of sticky tape.

'Mama . . .'

'Let's get inside. It's cold.'

Karen picked up the crushed box and ushered her mother inside. Instead of following Robert to the sitting room, Karen led her mother into the kitchen. She plucked two shot glasses and a bottle off a high shelf. 'Havana?'

A ghost of a smile played over Charlaine's lips. 'You know better than that, sweetie.'

Karen left the bottle and stooped to a low cupboard. When she straightened, she held a tall, unopened bottle of Wray and Nephew.

'That's my girl.'

She cracked the lid and poured a generous measure of rum into the shot glasses.

Charlaine didn't wait but tossed hers back. 'Wonderful. I needed that.'

Karen poured another. 'What's going on, Mama? You look tired. I wasn't sure you'd come tonight.'

'How could I not come see my baby girl's new house? And meet her friends?'

'You've met my friends. You know them. Cindy always asks after you.'

Charlaine frowned. 'And how do you tell her anything? You never call me. You never visit me.'

'Neither do you.'

Silence. They both drank.

Obnoxious rap lyrics floated through the open kitchen door. Someone shouted and the song cut short, replaced seconds later by a softer, reggae beat.

Karen gripped the bottle of rum. 'I hear Robert is making himself at home.'

'You mustn't hate him, sweetie. He's a good man.'

'Is he?'

'Of course he is.'

'And is he just good to you or does that extend to Suzanne? And Lola? And Catherine? And Lucy?'

With each name Charlaine shrank further and further into herself until she appeared low and broken in her chair. 'He's not seeing them any more.'

'So there's someone new?'

Charlaine stared into her shot glass.

'Mama?'

'It's just me. *Only* me and he cares for me now. I need that.'

'You survived without him for years.'

'I had you.'

A twinge of sadness plucked Karen's heart and brought a bitter taste to her mouth. 'You still do. You'll always have me.'

A tear gathered in Charlaine's eye and rolled down her cheek. She didn't bother to wipe it away. 'I won't.'

'Mama?'

'You've got this man now. Daniel. You've moved and you'll forget about me. There'll be nobody left to look after me when I can't manage any more.'

'What are you talking about?'

She looked up from the shot glass. The whites of her eyes were red, her cheeks puffy. 'I'm sick, sweetie. Cancer. It's terminal.'

DAN

'Hello?' Dan tapped his knuckles on the bathroom door.

A loud cough answered, followed by retching and the wet slap of something heavy hitting standing water. He rolled his eyes. 'Clean up when you're done, please.'

The door popped open. Cindy slid through. 'Have you got any mint tea or fennel?'

He cocked an eyebrow. 'Seriously?'

'Yeah. I don't drink that shit but Sam swears it will settle her stomach.'

'Now?'

She arched an eyebrow. 'Unless you want your bathroom to smell like puke and cookies for the rest of the night.' With that, Cindy darted back into the bathroom and slammed the door.

Dan rubbed his face with his hands.

Fuck me . . .

On his return to the kitchen, he paused to peer into the living room. The music wasn't any he recognised; a slow, Bob Marley sort of style. In the middle of the room, dancing with his mother, a tall, wrestler-wide black man in a pale grey suit, sang along at the top of his lungs.

Dan watched his mother sway to the music. He opened his mouth. Nothing came out.

What the actual fuck? Who's that?

The stranger pawed Maxine like a horny teenager, his thick, broad hands dwarfing her tiny waist. The hem of her floral dress slipped over her boney knees and climbed her thighs.

Dan reeled, like he'd spent too long on a roller-coaster. 'Mum?'

She turned. A sunny, half-crazed smile stretched her lips. 'Daniel, darling! What a wonderful party. I'm having a marvellous time. Have you met my new friend? This is—darn and blast it, I've forgotten your name.'

The man swept off his hat. A thick mane of dreadlocks tumbled out and kissed the small of his back. 'I'm Robert Owusu, my snow-queen.'

Dan's knees weakened. A stream of nausea rushed up from his belly, threatening to choke him. He gripped the door frame. 'Owusu?'

'That's right.' Robert turned. He loomed, like a cold, dark mountain. 'And *you're* Daniel. The one seeing mi little girl.'

Little girl?

'I'm Karen's boyfriend if that's what you mean.'

'You seem a little old for her, Silver Fox.'

Dan touched the streaks of grey in his hair. 'That's none of your business.'

'Daniel! So rude.' Maxine wobbled over, grabbed his hand and gave his wrist a firm slap. 'I taught you better than that.'

He jerked away and focused on Robert. 'You're Karen's dad?'

'Yes.'

'Her actual, blood father?'

Robert exhaled sharply. He seemed to grow taller still and spoke with all the menace of a grizzly bear. 'What are you saying, Silver Fox? You weren't expecting mi?'

Fuck, no.

He licked his lips. 'Where's Karen?'

Maxine shoved her way forward. 'No idea, Darling, but when you find her, tell her to bring out more of those wonderful chocolate chip cookies.'

'Please say you're joking.'

'I don't know why you hid them—naughty boy!—but I made sure everybody sampled them. I simply must have the recipe.'

Robert grinned, showing off a mouthful of gold teeth. They gleamed to match the sovereigns dangling from a thick chain around his neck. Another flashed on his left middle finger. 'Mi can help you with that my Ice Queen. Mi think maybe them cookies are a *special* kind. That right, Silver Fox?' Amusement seemed to strengthen his accent, broad Caribbean with a hint of something else.

Dan didn't answer. Couldn't. He backed off. 'I'll talk to you in a minute, Mum. Don't eat any more cookies.'

She waved her hand, an absent dismissal as she returned to dancing. As she swayed to the sensual music, Robert curled his arms around her waist to grind up close. Maxine giggled—actually giggled—and slipped her arms around his neck.

Dan choked on a surge of horror. *I can't watch this.*

He fled, stumbling into the kitchen and slamming the door behind him. His escape dulled the music to a low roar, but the pounding in his head continued.

Karen sat at the table, clutching her mother's hands. Tears streamed down her face.

'Your dad is outside.' The words didn't sound like his. Heat rose in his neck and jaw. He forced it down. 'Karen?'

She looked at him. Her eyes sparkled with tears. 'Dan . . .'

'Your *dad*, Kaz. Really? What the hell?'

'This isn't the time—'

He pounded his fist on the sideboard. Plates rattled on the draining rack. A tumbler fell into the sink. He didn't care. Two steps took him closer to the table. 'You told me your dad was dead.'

Charlaine winced. 'Sweetie, how could you?'

Karen leapt up, flinging her mother's hands away. She paced the room. 'He *is* dead to me. As far as I'm concerned that man died years ago. He shouldn't be here.'

'But he *is* here,' Dan snarled. 'In our living room. Mauling my stoned mother.'

'What?'

'Pete bought space-cakes—idiot!—and they're doing the rounds. I don't know how many she ate, but she's not herself.'

Karen gave her mother a pointed look then wiped her nose on the back of her wrist. 'Please, Dan, I know you're pissed off, but we'll talk about it later. Something bigger is going on.'

'Bigger than your dad coming back from the dead?'

'Mama has cancer,' Karen roared. Her hands shook. 'I'd say that's bigger than some womanising arsehole crashing our party.'

His ears rang; shrill, clanging bells that filled his head and blocked all other sound. The world pitched and dipped before him, shimmering as through scalding heat. He tried to speak, but his tongue stuck to the roof of his mouth. Only when Charlaine patted his hand, did he realise he had sat down.

'Cancer?' He barely recognised his voice. 'Wow.' He turned, seeking Karen. She stood nearby, arms folded tight, chin ducked down. When he reached for her, she leapt away.

'Don't.'

'Kaz, please.'

'Don't.' Louder this time, forced through tears. 'I need you to—I don't know what I need.'

'I'm so sorry.'

'I don't need your sorries; I need Mama not to have cancer.'

He gasped, hunching over the table. Words fought for freedom on the tip of his tongue, but none felt right. What was he supposed to say?

'Sweetie, it's okay. I've made peace with it.' Charlaine whispered, gaze pinned to the table top. 'I'm fine.'

'You're dying, Mama.'

'We all have to die.'

'But you can't. I need you.'

Dan felt sick. Helplessness washed over him until he could barely breathe.

Charlaine smiled. 'You've got Dan now. He'll look after you.'

A lump formed in Dan's throat. He swallowed but it stuck there, choking his words.

'Won't you?' Charlaine gazed at him, calm and steady.

In that moment Dan knew exactly what Karen would look like in twenty years. Both women shared quiet, constant intensity, flawless skin and fine beauty.

He clutched the edge of the table. Cleared his throat. 'Of course I will.'

With a choking sob, Karen flung herself at him. He braced for the impact in time to stop the chair toppling and he held her while she wept. Tears moistened his shoulder. Her laboured, erratic breaths filled his ear. All the while, she clung to him, body trembling. He stroked her hair and said nothing.

Charlaine gave a small nod. A warm rush of gratitude flooded his body.

I'll look after her. I'll give her anything she needs.

'I'm sorry to tell you like this, sweetie. But I couldn't get here by myself. Trains are too much for me now, but Robert said he'd bring me. He wanted to see you.'

Karen stiffened.

'Charlaine, your *husband* is in the living room. He's asking for Karen but I don't think she's ready to see him yet.'

The older woman nodded. 'You're probably right. Maybe I can keep him out of trouble.' She plodded from the room, tugging on the door behind her. It swung back, slightly ajar, letting a trickle of noise through.

Karen moaned against the damp patches on his shirt. 'Dan, I'm so sorry. I didn't know he was coming. I would have said something sooner but Mama was so upset. Then we got talking and she told me. Oh God, cancer. Cancer! She's going to die.'

He chose not to speak, simply guiding Karen to the floor where he could hold them both without falling. She curled into his lap, tucking her knees to her chest and resting her head against his shoulder. One hand toyed with the curls of hair hanging over the back of his collar.

'I'm sorry, Kaz.' So inadequate.

'I know. Me too.'

'You've got nothing to be sorry about.'

'I should have told you about Robert. I hate that you had to meet him like that.'

He bit his lip. 'It was . . . unsettling.'

'Did he hurt you?'

'What? No.' The dry, rasping sensation returned to his mouth. 'Is he violent?'

'No, he doesn't like other men around his women.'

'You're his daughter.'

'That still counts.'

'He called me 'Silver Fox'.'

A bubble of laughter slid from Karen's mouth. 'Seriously? Hypocrite.'

'I saw his hair. I'm greyer than he is.'

'The locs?' she snorted. 'He's been dying those things since he was my age. He's greyer than a skunk's arse.'

Dan smiled. 'Shall I send everyone home?'

A split-second hesitation. 'No. That's not how I want to deal with this. Besides, people are having fun.'

'I don't care about everyone else. I love *you*.' The words slid off his tongue as though greased. So different to a few months ago when he could barely think them.

'I know, but they should stay. Let's build happy memories here.'

'We'll have plenty of happy things to remember. No rush.'

'But what if there is?' She lowered her knees and swivelled to face him. 'Mama was always so healthy. She's a yoga instructor for Christ's sake. If *she* has cancer any one of us could drop dead any moment.'

He cupped her face. 'How is that any different from an hour ago?'

Karen frowned.

'Kaz, nothing can prepare you for news like this, but you can't let it scare you out of living. We're all going to kick it at some point, just like Charlaine said. But we get to choose how we spend the time we have.'

Tears sparkled on her cheeks. He wiped them away with the pad of his thumb.

'I love you so much, Dan.'

'I know.' He kissed her nose. 'And I'll always be here, no matter what happens. Just tell me what you want me to do.'

A steady stare. 'Really?'

'Tell me what you need.'

'Kiss me.'

He grinned. 'I can do that.'

'Make me forget.'

Dan felt a flutter of panic. Forget the horrific news of mere minutes ago? How? What could possibly do that?

Gaze hot on his, Karen bit her lip. Her eyebrows twitched and she pressed her head against his chest again. Each hot breath billowed through his shirt and stroked his nipples.

'Please, Dan.' The begging note intensified. 'I'm so scared. I want to feel safe again, just for a little while.' Her lips quivered against his. More damp patches blossomed on his shirt.

'Please!' She pressed her lips to his, quick, desperate kisses as she tangled her hands in his hair.

I know this . . .

Karen gave a tiny whimper as she pulled back, her eyes bright with tears.

He growled, low in his throat. Understanding dawned, flashing in his mind like a stun grenade. 'Open your legs,' he murmured.

She stared at him. Smiled. Though she never spoke, her eyes screamed 'thank you'. She lowered herself on to his lap, hips pressed to his stomach, legs on either side of his thighs.

He ran his hands up and down her jeans. She twitched beneath his touch. 'You've got too many clothes on. We'll make do. Take your top off.'

Instant obedience. Never once breaking eye contact, she yanked the garment free and tossed it behind her. Again her breathing became unsteady, this time a product of arousal.

Dan held the moment, not touching, not moving, just looking.

She's so beautiful . . .

The smallest of groans rumbled at the back of her throat.

He traced a finger across the top of each breast, following the lines of her bra. When she sucked in a sharp breath, he pinched her nipples through the lacy cups, harder and harder until she cried out.

'Quiet. We have guests.'

She bit her lip.

'I want you to open the fridge and bring me the thinnest carrot you can find from the chill drawer.'

Her eyes widened. 'Seriously?'

'Do it.'

She hesitated, but again only for a moment. Dan took the chance to unfasten his trousers and pull his wakening member over the top of his boxers. By the time Karen returned, he was almost hard. He patted his lap. 'Sit.'

As she wriggled into place, Dan arranged his cock to stand up between them. He took the carrot and guided Karen's hands down to hold him. 'Make me come,' he told her. 'Hands only.'

'But—'

Dan wedged the carrot into her mouth. 'Make me come and keep that in your mouth. When we're done I want to put it back in the fridge, so no teeth marks, understand?'

A soft groan came from behind the carrot along with a muffled, 'I can't do that.'

'You can. Now be a good girl and jerk me off.'

It hurt at first, with no lube and sweat-damp fingers. He distracted himself by playing with her breasts, alternating between stroking and pinching her nipples. They hardened beneath his rough attention, visible as two round nubs against the lace. He hooked one breast free and squeezed it, dotting quick little nips all over it.

Soon a dribble of saliva fell from the corner of her lips and onto the head of his cock. She used it like lube, increasing her efforts while her soft moans grew louder.

The door to the kitchen hung slightly open. Shadows from the guests beyond flickered in and out of sight. The music changed to 80s glam rock.

He whispered in her ear. 'Do you think they can see us? Think they can see you whimpering like a bitch in heat as you stroke me? Maybe they'll enjoy the show. What do you think?' He freed the second soft mound from the confines of her bra and lathed his tongue over the pebble-hard nipple. When she arched her back and paused in her stroking, he bit down on it.

'God, Sir—'

'Hush. Keep working.'

As she did, he unfastened her pants. She grunted.

'You didn't think I was going to make it easy?'

Within seconds his fingers wriggled inside her underwear, seeking the hot, moist flesh there. She writhed against him, bucking her hips against his touch.

'Didn't take you long to get wet, did it? Or is this from when I had you swinging from the ceiling? God you're so fucking dirty, Kaz.'

She groaned again and twisted her hips until his index finger sank deep into her creamy centre. He let her control the penetration, waiting until she was fully impaled before adding a second finger.

'No teeth marks on that carrot, remember. If you bite it I'll have to find somewhere else to stick it.'

Karen thrashed against his fingers. Her breath hissed through clenched teeth, whispering over his face in hot, rhythmic gusts. Her hands moved faster.

Loud voices floated through the door.

'Hurry up Kaz. I won't let you come until you finish me off and if you don't, you're done until later tonight.'

She flashed him a deadly look, but increased the pace, adding a twist of her wrist as she drooled saliva all over her hands.

He rubbed his wet fingers over her lips, painting with her own slick juices. 'You look great like this. Maybe we should get a bridle gag. Would you like that? Or maybe a ring gag, holding you wide open so I can fuck your sexy mouth whenever I want.'

The carrot snapped. Chunks of orange vegetable flew across the room.

He grinned. 'Uh oh.'

Karen jerked free and slid down his lap, lying on her stomach between his legs and slurping his cock into her mouth.

Dan gasped and rocked his hips off the floor. The unexpected heat and moisture dragged him to the brink and shoved him over the edge. Stars exploded across his vision in green, blue and red. He grasped her hair, thrusting deep into her willing throat as his release barrelled through him.

Holy fucking hell!

When he finally relaxed and slumped against the cupboards, every limb hummed with weakness. Karen sat up, thumbing moisture off the corner of her mouth. She licked her lips.

He shook his head at her still fighting for breath. 'You snapped the carrot. Big trouble, little kitten.'

Karen crawled up his body, feasting a kiss on his lips. He could taste himself on her, a salty, musky mix of her pleasure and his.

'I'll clean the bits.'

'Good girl.'

She hopped away and scooped up the carrot chunks. He watched her do it while fastening his trousers. He stood. Her scent lingered on his fingers and he took a moment to sniff. Arousal pulsed in his sensitive cock, but he tamped it down.

Now the moment was over he remembered what started it. Charlaine's thin, weary face swam across his vision. 'Kaz? You okay?'

She faced him, dropping a handful of carrot chunks onto the table. 'You understand me, Dan. You know what I need. You don't ask questions, you just *do*. That's all I need to get me through tonight. Tomorrow is another matter but tonight . . . I'm okay.'

He watched her face, searching for some sign of sadness, or discomfort. He found none, just a small, satisfied smile. 'You didn't get to come.'

She shrugged. 'It gives me something to look forward to.'

'Karen—'

'I'm fine, Dan. I need to find Robert before he mauls anyone. Else.' She swept out of the room, tugging her top back on as she went.

Dan stayed behind, staring at the sink. His breath rushed out in a long, harsh gasp and he clutched the sink with both hands. A small piece of carrot rolled to rest against his thumb. His eyes burned. Knuckles whitened. As the first salty drops splashed the back of his hands, he lowered his head, squeezing his eyes shut.

Fuck . . .

KAREN

Karen walked back into the living room with her head held high and her heart stampeding in her chest. She aimed for Cindy, loitering near the buffet table with her arm wrapped around Sam who still looked ragged around the edges.

'Hey,' she sidled closer.

'Where the hell is your idiot Dom?' Cindy cut a glance at her. 'Half an hour ago I told him I needed tea. Now the bathroom stinks, the toilet is blocked and Sam still can't stand.'

'Sorry. We were in the kitchen. Talking.'

Cindy's eyes narrowed. She stepped back and looked her up and down. 'What happened?'

'Nothing.'

'Bullshit, bitch. You've been crying. Spit it out.'

'Please, Cindy, not now.'

'Is it Robert? Why is he even here? I thought he ran off with that belly dancer from Sussex.'

'So did I.'

'So it's not him. What's wrong? Is it Dan again? Do I need to break his knee caps?'

Karen clutched her hair. 'No! Jesus, give it a rest, will you? I'll tell you later, okay?'

Cindy looked ready to argue, but at that moment Sam unfurled herself and planted a deep, searching kiss on her lips. When she came up for air she stroked her fingers through Cindy's ice white tresses. 'I need tea. Can you get me tea? I'd really, really like some tea. Tea.'

Cindy sighed. 'God, I love it when you're stoned. Yes, I'll get you some tea.' To Karen she added, 'Keep an eye on her. This is a stronger hit than I usually give her.' She marched off.

Karen took Sam by the arm and guided her back to the sofa. 'Sit with me.'

Sam lurched a step forward then fell straight back onto the cushions. She spread her arms across the back and gave an inane grin. 'You know, nobody ever tells you how pretty you are. I hope Dan realises what a lucky man he is.'

She smiled. 'He knows.'

'Your hair too, all puffy, black and curly. I used to wish mine would do that. You'd think it might since my dad is as black as you. But no, I got this boring straight shit. Maybe he isn't even my dad.'

Half listening, Karen sought her own father. He fiddled with the stereo, his back to Charlaine who spoke over him with big, angry hand gestures.

Sam grabbed her shoulder. 'They say children often worry about turning into their parents. Either they aim for it or they panic about it. Do you ever consider that your relationship with Dan is what you *wish* your mum had with your dad?'

Stunned, Karen sat back. 'How many cookies *did* you eat?'

'Twelve.' She giggled. 'Don't tell Cindy. But Dan looks after you, doesn't he? In everything. All you have to do is what you're told.'

Wary of the crowd, Karen scooted closer. 'Keep it down. No one knows.'

'I do. Cindy does. Pete too.'

Yes, more's the pity.

Karen caught a glimpse of him on the other side of the room. When he saw her, he looked away.

'He fancies you.' Sam twirled a piece of hair around her finger.

'Pete? No way. He's Dan's friend.'

'He saw you naked.'

Karen thought back to the cage, to Pete's hot, searching gaze all over her body. She groaned. 'Don't remind me.'

'I'm just saying . . . maybe he thinks that gives him some sort of claim. He's been watching you all night.'

A shiver of cold rippled down her spine. 'Really?'

'Like a dog eyeing a bone. Kinda creepy.'

Karen looked again, this time under the pretence of waving at her neighbours. On the peripherals of her vision Pete stared at her, his brow furrowed into a deep frown. His right hand clasped a bottle of beer, the knuckles hard and white.

He is watching me. Shit.

She picked at a join in the sofa. 'What should I do?'

Sam interrupted her intense study of the back of her hand to give a lazy, one-shouldered shrug. 'Simple, isn't it? Tell Dan.'

'I can't. They're friends.'

'He won't hear it from anyone else. Don't you think he should know? Wow . . .' she giggled. 'I have loads of scars on my hands.'

'Sam! Focus.'

'I am. Look, that's when I fell off my bike—I was ten. This one was Mittens; I hated that cat. This one was Cindy. She bought me a ring but it was too small. The hospital had to cut it off.'

'Sam, please.' Karen grabbed her hands and waited until she looked up. 'I know you're stoned, but you need to talk to me. I can't tell Dan, okay? They're best friends.'

Another shrug. 'Then tell Cindy. She'll fix it.'

She would, but that's not an option if Pete ever wants to fit another shop front.

'No. And don't you say a word either.'

Sam lolled back against the sofa. 'Fine. Fine, fine, fine . . .' She trailed off into a low, distant humming, tracing more scars on the backs of her hands.

I need a drink.

She leapt up. Dodging well-wishing neighbours and colleagues she grabbed a plastic cup off the table and a half-empty bottle of cheap vodka. She poured a double and knocked it back. Then another.

'Everything okay, Kaz?' Pete appeared at her side. He didn't look at her, not fully, but placed his hand on her shoulder. His grip was warm, fingers tight on her skin.

She eased away. 'I'm fine.'

'You've been crying.'

She peered into his face. A whiff of beer-breath puffed across her nostrils, hot and sour. 'And *you've* been drinking.'

'So? It's a party.'

'That's right. *My* party. I'll cry if I want to.'

'Touché.' He snagged a handful of peanuts from a dish and crammed them into his mouth. 'Can I talk to you for a second? Alone?'

The request tied her stomach in knots. The thought of being alone with him sent lines of cold racing up and down her spine. They hadn't been alone since the cage incident.

Until that moment Karen never realised how tall he was. How big. His arms, thick and knotted with muscle from all that hard labour. He gazed at her, close enough that every breath caused his chest to brush her arm.

'I don't think that's a good idea.'

'It will only take a second. Out there.' He gestured to the door of the living room.

'But—'

'He's not here, Karen. Can't he spare you for three seconds so we can talk? Or are you so into this slave thing that you can't make up your own mind?'

Unease melted beneath a rush of irritation. 'He doesn't own me.'

'Then come talk to me. Two minutes.' He walked out.

From her position on the sofa Sam began to giggle, a shrill, constant, most un-Sam-like sound.

Karen walked passed her, following Pete's retreating back as he aimed for the garden.

On the way Karen heard the disgusted voice of someone in the downstairs bathroom and the burbling of a toilet refusing to flush. A sickly smell permeated the hallway and she held her nose as Pete led her out the back door.

Outside, with the cool crispness of October tugging at her clothes, she wrapped both arms around herself and waited. 'Well?'

'I got you a present.'

She froze. 'Why?' The word was sharper than she intended, but she couldn't help it.

'Call it a housewarming gift. I saw it and thought of you.' He reached down to the floor near the sliding doors and held up a small plastic bag.

Karen didn't take it, wondering instead, when he had the time to come and plant this little 'gift.'

He hunched his shoulders. 'At least look before you reject me.'

Moonlight caught the links of her slave band as she reached for the bag. Inside fluttered the creamy pages of a thick, dusty paperback. When she pulled it out and looked at the cover her hands began to tremble. 'Where did you get this?'

Pete scratched the back of his neck. 'There's a bookshop near my workshop. They're closing down so I went in. Not for me, but, you know . . . some of my friends like books.'

She stroked the weathered cover, then opened it. The musty scent of aged paper billowed up on a cloud of dust. 'This is a first edition.'

'I know. The guy in the shop said that's a good thing. I just thought you'd prefer this cover to the newer looking ones. They seem tacky.'

Karen looked again at the battered copy of 'Alice in Wonderland'. Her fingers trembled as she turned the delicate pages. 'I loved this book as a child.'

'I know. You told Dan, really, but I remember. We were sitting in the kitchen at Dan's old place. You made this weird, lumpy pork thing and called it meatloaf. It looked disgusting, but tasted amazing. You've not made it since.'

Karen grinned at the memory. 'I must have used every scrap of meat left in the fridge. I can't even remember how I did it.'

He stared into her eyes. 'It was gorgeous.'

She clutched the book to her chest. 'Thank you, Pete. This is really sweet of you.' With a quick step forward, she hugged him. An impulsive move for sure. She'd never touched him that way in the past, but the gesture of the book and his uncertain expression brought it out of her.

Pete relaxed beneath her touch, running his hands down her back. 'I wanted to do something for you. I wanted to show you that I'm just as good.'

Warning bells clanged. She tried to pull back, but his grip tightened, both hands now holding her against his body.

'I'm just as good as Dan, Kaz. Why can't you see?' He pushed his lips to hers, fighting to part them with a thrust of his tongue. The taste of lager exploded in her mouth and she jerked her head back with a cry.

'Pete, get off me.'

He gripped tighter. 'Just give me a chance. I can control you too. That's what you want, isn't it?' Another kiss. This time he held the back of her head with one hand and pinned her arms with the other. His tongue wormed in.

Karen squirmed, jerking her head from side to side. Nothing. She may well have punched an elephant for all the effect it had. Panic seared through her. Breathing quickened.

'Get off!'

His free hand left her arms and slipped beneath her blouse, grabbing for her breasts. She drew her leg back, ready to kick him.

'Now what's this then?' A voice speared out of the dark.

Pete thrust her away so hard, she stumbled and fell. The book flew from her hands and landed in the grass.

Robert stood in the open doorway, a fat, unlit cigar hanging from the side of his mouth.

Pete swallowed hard enough to be heard over the thud of music from within. 'I—'

"You—' 'you—" Robert mocked. "You' what?' He tilted his head so the brim of his hat left a thick shadow across his eyes. 'Thought you'd manhandle mi girl while nobody was looking?'

'It's not like that,' snapped Karen. She got as far as her knees before he thrust a hand in her direction, a silent order to shut up.

'Well, I see you, boy,' Robert continued. 'I know a man who likes the ladies—I'm one myself. But mi girl there, she not for you. She got more class than the likes of you or I.'

A crimson flush crept up Pete's neck and jaw. He opened his mouth but no words came out. In the end he puffed up his chest and growled low at the back of his throat. 'Class? Yeah, real classy giving a blow job on the kitchen floor with guests less than ten feet away.'

Karen felt like he'd slapped her. She scrambled to her feet and shoved him in the chest. 'You were watching? What's wrong with you?'

'That's what you like isn't it? An audience? Sharing? I don't see why all these other people can be involved but *I'm* not good enough to—' he looked away.

Silence loomed, broken occasionally by the low boom of bass from the speakers within.

'Baby-girl, what is this idiot talking about?'

'Shut up, Papa!' As she finished speaking, Karen had no idea who was more shocked, Robert or herself. But the word was out now and she couldn't take it back. She faced the easier target. 'Pete, we need to talk about this, but not now. Do you understand? *Not now.*'

He wiped his mouth. 'When then? You never talk to me any more. Every time I'm in the room you make an excuse to run. I'm not the one who hits you, so why am I the monster?'

The world shrank to a tiny dot. Low buzzing filled her ears. Karen gasped, but the breath caught in her throat to leave her dizzy and light-headed.

Robert swelled like an overripe fruit. He jerked the hat off and tossed it on the ground. 'Hits you? Who? Does he mean the skinny little Silver Fox in there?'

'Shut up! Fuck, just go away, Robert, please.' Switching back to his true name meant nothing. They both knew it.

'Is that man hitting you?'

'Go away!'

He gave a curt nod. 'Go away, you say. I'll go, but we'll talk. No one hits mi baby-girl, understand? I'll break their spine first.'

'Papa, please!' Desperation changed her pleas. 'Leave me alone.'

'We'll talk,' he muttered. 'And I'm watching *you,* too.' With a last hard glare at Pete, he returned to the house.

Pete stared at his toes.

Karen slapped him, one solid crack to the side of his face. 'What the fuck?' she roared. 'Are you insane? Do you go blurting everybody's sexual deviances to their parents?'

'Sorry, I—'

She hit him again. 'No, Pete. No 'sorry'. I have too much going on right now to stand here and hold your fucking hand while you crush on me. This is the way it is: I'm with Dan, not you. The relationship Dan and I have is exactly that, *his* and *mine*. What we choose to do with it is none of your fucking business, is that clear?'

'But he's so selfish. It's always about him—does he even care what you want?'

She hit him a third time, a full punch that made her entire hand throb. 'Fuck you,' she snarled. 'You don't get to ask that. Get out. You're not going back in there, just leave. Use the back gate.'

'Karen—'

'Get out! And take your book.' She whirled away from him, yanking open the door in time to hear a loud shout came from the living room and the crunch of breaking glass.

DAN

Dan reached the door to the kitchen as Cindy arrived on the other side. She saw the tea, frowned and shoved him back into the room. The door slammed. 'What's going on with you and Karen?'

He put the mug down and shoved his hands into his pockets. 'Nothing. Why?'

'She's out there moping like a kicked puppy. I know you guys have your problems, all couples do, but I can't handle seeing her like that. She's like a sister to me. If you've done something, I swear I'll rip out your pubes and use them to stuff a cushion.'

'Colourful and direct as ever, Cindy. I haven't done anything. If she hasn't told you herself then she's not ready for you to know.'

'Bullshit. She tells me everything.'

'Maybe she needs time to deal with it first.'

'Was it Robert?'

Dan's hands tightened in his pockets. 'You know about him?'

'Of course.'

'She told me he was dead.'

Cindy's eyebrows shot up toward her hairline. 'Yeah? Fucked up.'

'I know.'

'She sometimes might wish he was—the way he treats Charlaine—but the creep is very much alive. And he's taken a shine to your mother.'

He raised his hands. 'I'm trying not to think about that. Apparently space-cakes squeeze the racist dowager right out of her.'

'Well something had to loosen her up.' She grinned. 'Come on, Dan. Tell me. Maybe she's testing you. Maybe she did it on purpose. She must know I'd ask. I'm supposed to be getting tea for Sam.'

Dan nudged the mug towards her. 'Then why don't you take it and stop pestering me into telling you things I shouldn't?'

'Did she say don't tell me?'

He hesitated.

'Exactly. Tell me. I'll find out eventually.

Dan glanced at the door, drumming his fingertips against the counter. 'You can't tell anybody else.'

'Fine, just tell me what's wrong with my friend.'

'Charlaine has cancer.'

Cindy froze. She barely breathed. 'Fuck off.'

'I'm serious.'

'Damn. That woman is the healthiest human being I've ever known. No wonder Karen's a mess. Why aren't you sending everyone home?'

'She told me not to.'

'Always the idiot.' Cindy leaned against the counter and trailed her finger through a puddle of wine. 'You'd better look after her, Dan. She's going to need you.'

He bit his lip over a scathing response. Instead he said, 'I look after her just fine.'

'Then why are you here while she's out there?'

Too much. Every barb, every threat of violence, no matter how comic, finally became too much. He leaned down, using their height difference to his advantage. 'Because I just ordered her to give me a hand job and now she needs recovery time.'

A slow smile claimed Cindy's lips. She stared at him for long, intense seconds before backing off. 'Maybe you *do* know her. Forget I said anything. Pervert.' With that last jab, she grabbed the mug of tea and swept out of the kitchen.

Dan exhaled and wandered over to the fridge. He opened it and gazed inside without seeing. The air swirled over his face and arms until goosebumps peppered his skin.

The kitchen door opened and an unfamiliar face looked through. He paused in the doorway before giving a brief thumbs up. 'Great party, man.' The man slouched away.

Dan slammed the fridge shut and sat at the table. In his mind's eye he saw Karen again, face streaked with tears. He longed to hold her, to kiss her soft cheeks and wipe away the glimmering drops with the pad of his thumb.

But I can't. She won't let me.

On his feet again. Stopping at the site of their latest mini scene to relive her delicate touch.

'Fuck it,' he snarled, stomping from the kitchen and back into the living room. He aimed straight for his father, seeking comfort in his calm and unflappable exterior.

Julian met him with a pat on the back and a small smile. 'You okay, my boy?'

'Fine, Dad. Where's Mum?'

'Somewhere. Probably snooping the rest of your walls and carpets.'

Dan grunted, but said nothing. He had no fear of her finding anything she shouldn't; everything was very well hidden. 'The spare room isn't ready yet, but if you tell me when you want it I'll make the bed.'

'No, no, we aren't staying here. Maxine booked us a hotel.'

Dan paused his scanning of the crowd. 'What?'

'We figured you'd want some alone time with Karen.'

'That's never bothered Mum before.'

Julian smiled. 'She's paying a bit more attention to my ideas at the moment. Besides there's a tea room close by and she's adamant we have brunch there.'

Dan laughed. 'Thank goodness. I couldn't cope if I thought she actually wanted to give me space.'

'She loves you, Daniel. That's all.'

He thought again of Charlaine's devastating news. He caught sight of her from the corner of his eye and promised never again to whine about his mother. Who knew how long he'd have her. She was far older than Charlaine and less health-conscious, despite her airs and graces.

'I know, Dad.' He clapped his father on the shoulder and turned, in time to meet Robert marching in from another room. He stumbled as the bigger man barrelled into him, chest first. He skipped back to avoid crushed toes.

'You been hitting mi daughter, big man?' he snarled.

Dan felt sick. He looked up—and up—into those narrowed eyes and tried to wet his mouth enough to speak.

Robert's sheer bulk forced him against the snack table which creaked under his weight. 'Well? Talk to mi, yuh piece of filth.'

Dan found his voice. With effort. 'No.'

'Really?'

'Of course he doesn't.' Julian stepped forward, his hands raised palm out. 'Where would you get a ridiculous idea like that?'

'Stay out of this, snowy. I'm talking to this skinny creep.'

'This 'skinny creep' is my son.'

Dan touched his shoulder. 'It's okay, Dad. I've got this. Robert—' One look at the bigger man's face changed his approach. 'Mr Owusu, I don't know what you've heard or who you've been speaking to, but I've never hurt your daughter. Ask her yourself.'

'I just came from her. She said otherwise.'

'Karen did?' He failed to keep the shock from his voice. 'That's ridiculous. There must be some mistake.'

'You calling mi girl a liar?'

'No, I—'

'Me then?'

'No!'

'I won't be called a liar to mi face. Not by the likes of you.'

Stars exploded in front of Dan's eyes. The world tipped upside down and he caught a vague impression of a fist flying passed his face before he hit something hard. It gave beneath him and dumped him on the floor along with food and half-full cups of beer and fizzy drinks. A smashing sound, then a wash of thin, red liquid washed over his chest and shoulder. Impact against the floor jarred his neck and back and a stab of pain raced up and down his spine. His fingers brushed a sharp edge.

What the . . .

When he next opened his eyes, he saw dozens of shoes and a pair of shiny black boots an inch away from his nose. Someone screamed. A shrill voice cried 'Don't!' Another sound, like a roar, rolled over him, then the air exploded with loud voices. The scent of crushed grass and mud filled his nose and the black boots slammed down near his face.

A dull rush of pain lanced up and down the right side of his jaw. The world began to blur. Sounds of a scuffle filtered through, then a filthy pair of steel toe boots appeared, battered and dotted with white paint.

Distantly, Dan knew those shoes and their owner, but the buzzing in his ears prevented him from naming him.

He rolled onto his back and saw the shattered remains of the snack table. A frantic voice called his name. Something grabbed his legs and pulled. The debris vanished and bright light speared his eyes.

'Dan!'

'What?' An explosion of pain blossomed in his jaw. He didn't try to speak again.

Then Karen appeared, her beautiful face fuzzy and uneven. He reached out to touch her and saw his fingers perform the same wobbling, blurring dance.

'Dan, can you sit up? Can you see me? How many fingers am I holding up?'

He blinked. 'Six.'

'On one hand? Shit, Dan, try again. How many?'

He squeezed his eyes shut then looked again. The world swam. Colours bled into each other. Then, with a snap, the images rocked together into one solid whole. 'Two,' he said with confidence. As the word left his mouth, his jaw creaked in protest, fresh pain spreading from his chin to the top of his head.

'Oh, God, that hurts!'

'Shh, don't talk. Come on, stand up.'

Several hands tugged his sleeves. He stood and found Karen beneath his arm, supporting his weight. His father stood opposite, holding the other arm across his shoulders.

'What happened?' he managed, blinking through waves of pain.

No answer. Just a sea of stunned faces.

'Talk to me.' On his feet, his thoughts were less foggy. He looked up. Remembered Robert. But the big man was nowhere in sight. But he could hear him. Shouting. Threatening. Calling his name.

Suddenly his jaw didn't hurt so much. 'What happened to Robert?'

Karen tightened her grip on his waist. 'Pete kicked him out.'

'Pete? Why? What happened?'

'He punched you, Dan. I think you were actually out of it for a second or two. I'm so sorry. This is my fault.'

'No . . .' That didn't seem right. 'You didn't do anything.'

'If Pete hadn't run in I don't know what would have happened. Robert was going to kick your head in.'

Dan remembered the black shoes so close to his face. The scuffed work boots.

His stomach gave a little flutter.

'I'm taking you upstairs.' Karen walked on, forcing him to join her, slow, but steady. By the time they reached the door, Dan's vision was no longer blurred. Only then did he notice the silence in the room.

Almost silence.

The music no longer played and the living room was thick with tension. But through it all, on the edges of his hearing he heard soft laughter. With effort he turned his head.

Sam sat on the sofa, a steaming mug in her hands. Her shoulders bucked as she tried, without success, to keep the giggles in. Beside her, rubbing her shoulders, sat Cindy, for once, utterly serious.

Could this evening get any more fucked up?

Upstairs, he let Karen lower him into bed.

Julian tugged off his shoes. 'Don't let him fall asleep, my dear.' He brushed off his hands and smoothed back his hair. 'He's a tough lad, but so is your father. Look out for concussion. Keep him awake for at least an hour and watch his eyes. If he gets dizzy or sick call me, okay?'

Karen wiped her cheeks with the flat of her palms. She spoke clear and firm, but Dan knew her well enough to recognise the tremor in her voice. 'I'll look after him.'

'Dad,' he began.

'No.' Julian raised his hand. 'We'll talk tomorrow. Maybe in the afternoon? I'll make sure everyone leaves and then I'll lock up. You stay here.'

He longed to argue, but the pain returned to his jaw and could no longer be ignored. Every time he moved his head, colours swam before his eyes and pain raced around his skull. 'Fine.' Only when he heard the door click shut did he realise he'd closed his eyes. He didn't bother opening them. 'Kaz?'

The bed sank on his left side, then Karen was there, her soft hands stroking his face. He smelled the faint sweetness of her cocoa butter moisturiser and the mint oils she used to soften her hair.

'Kaz . . . what a colossal fuck up.'

'I know, I'm sorry. It went so wrong so fast, I didn't mean for him to find out.'

Dan waved his hand around until she grasped it. 'Whatever you said, this isn't your fault. None of this is your fault.' It hurt to speak, but he felt compelled to say it. 'Robert is—I don't know. But don't blame yourself for his actions. I get the feeling you've done plenty of that in your time.'

She stroked his hair. 'Don't you go all social worker on me, Daniel Scotney.'

He laughed. It hurt, but he did it anyway. 'Sorry. Just, please, don't blame yourself. *He's* the crazy one.'

'Is that a professional term?'

'The professional term is 'fucking nut-bag' but I'll stick with lay terms for you.'

He opened his eyes in time to see her lean forward, pressing a tender kiss to the side of his face.

'You're going to have a huge bruise in the morning.'

'Makes a change.'

She smirked. 'I have more fun getting my bruises.'

'Ain't that the truth.' He tried to sit up, but it was half an effort. She put a hand on his chest to ease him back into place and unbuttoned his shirt.

'We need a new table,' she mused. 'And a punch bowl.'

'Broken?'

'Smashed to bits. He *really* hit you.'

He tried to recall, but the memory remained blurred. 'I didn't see it coming. One second I was standing, the next—' he groaned. 'This really hurts.'

'I'll get some ice.' Karen vanished, leaving him to watch the shadows from the trees outside play across the ceiling. She returned and pressed a rustling pack to the side of his face.

'Peas,' she said. 'The ice is all gone.'

'Thanks.' He held it in place with one hand while she pulled off his sopping wet shirt. Then trousers. She left his boxers and snuggled up beside him, resting her head on his chest.

'What a shitty night,' she murmured.

'Tell me about it.'

KAREN

Karen woke suddenly without knowing why. Sunlight speared her eyes and she groaned, rolling left to bury her face in Dan's chest. Her cheek struck empty sheets.

In an instant she was fully awake, bolt upright and searching the room. 'Dan?' Memory of the night before returned in snatches. The party. Her mother's terrible news. Pete. Her father. Dan.

She tumbled out of bed in a sprawl of duvet, kicking her way free and rushing to the door. 'Dan!' Just before she hurried down the stairs, the toilet flushed. Whirling round, she ran for the bathroom, blundering through the door without knocking.

Dan stood at the sink, hands dripping water. Aside from a bemused expression he wore nothing else.

She threw herself at him, wrapped both arms around his neck and squeezed while tears slipped down her cheeks. The panic of moments ago eased. 'Where did you go? You scared me.'

He stroked her hair. 'I needed a whizz. It *is* morning.'

'You were hurt. I thought you might be lying somewhere all unconscious and concussed.'

'A bit irrational, wouldn't you say?'

Perhaps, but Dan didn't know Robert like she did. He couldn't know what the big man was capable of. She settled for a sullen, 'Screw you.'

Dan kissed her on the cheek. 'I'm fine.' He dried his hands.

For the first time she saw his face. The left side of his jaw blossomed black and blue, mottled like the back of a whale. His cheek swelled until the lower lid of his left eye squeezed almost shut and a faint trail of bruising marched up the side of his face.

'Jesus.'

'I know.' He turned to the mirror for another look. 'He only hit me once. What is he, a wrestler?'

Karen shook her head. 'Boxer.'

'Really?'

'For years before I was born. He switched to training when Mama was pregnant. He won awards, but when I arrived it all stopped. I don't think he ever really forgave me for messing up his career.' She visualised her father as he once looked. Narrow in the waist and broad across the shoulders, his ears and nose misshapen from several maulings. He stood in the study, what he liked to call the 'Trophy Room' staring at newspaper clippings, medals and trophies.

'It's not your fault, Kaz.'

'You've said that a lot recently.'

'Well it's not.'

'Tell him that, would you?' Satisfied that Dan was alive, conscious and speaking, she put the seat down on the toilet so she could sit. 'Julian said Robert thought you hit me. That's why he punched you. Idiot.'

'He was protecting you.'

'His time to do that is long gone. He's just an arsehole.'

Dan fumbled his toothbrush from the pot on the edge of the sink. 'What I can't figure out is where he got the idea in the first place. He was fine before that, grinding against my mum like a randy pit-bull. Next time I see him, I beat my girlfriend. I mean, what?'

Karen gazed at the floor. She bunched her fists on her knees and tried to think of a way to explain that wouldn't lead to more punching, shouting and general casualties. 'Pete let slip that we're kinky.'

'Excuse me?' The words came out garbled and wet. Dan faced her with a mouth full of foam, toothbrush hanging from the side of his mouth.

'We were in the garden, he gave me a housewarming present and he—'

I can't tell him about the kiss.

She cleared her throat. 'We were talking about . . . the house and—and stuff. Robert overheard a bunch of stuff he shouldn't have and when I told him we'd talk about it, he stormed off. I didn't know he'd go straight for you.'

'Wow.' More bubbles frothed from Dan's mouth.

'But Pete . . . we were talking about subbing and the library and . . .'

'What?' Dan's words were clear, the toothpaste gone. Swallowed. 'No wonder your dad went crazy. It sounds awful to someone who doesn't know the facts. Jesus. Pete is an idiot sometimes.'

'He didn't mean to. It slipped out.' Karen had no idea why she defended Pete. She just knew that she couldn't bear the thought of Dan knowing the truth. 'He was angry and jealous.'

Dan shook his head and wandered back into the bedroom. He pulled a pair of boxers from the drawers. 'Jealous, though? You see it too. I didn't think you paid that much attention to him.'

Karen frowned. 'Well . . . he was pretty plain about it.'

'He's giving you an earful too? If he's so bothered about us having a good time maybe he should join Kink4Life. I'll bet he could find a great Domme to look after him.'

'What?'

'You know about his latent submissive tendencies, right? He hides it well, but all that fuss about Pizza Express . . . what else could it be? I wish he'd admit it. He'd be happier if he did.'

Karen thought about correcting him, but the thought of Pete's hands all over her body cut her short.

He doesn't need to know all that.

She decided to link the subject to their talk of the evening before. 'You could suggest a Domme for him. Or I could find him one. I know lots of female dominants through Kink4Life.'

He grinned as he wriggled into the boxers. 'Getting tips, are you?'

'Sure. I'll need them one day.'

'Yes, Hannah told me what you did last time you had her alone. I think she likes where this is going. Wherever that is.'

'She told me there are male subs looking for a new Domme. Nothing big or high maintenance, just an *every now and then* sort of deal.'

'Do you know anyone?'

She watched his face. 'I was thinking *I* could help them out.'

He paused. 'How?'

'By being their temporary Domme.'

'But you're a sub.'

'I can be both. Ever heard of a Switch?'

'Sure, but you're not a Switch. You're my delicious, tasty, obedient, sexy sub who—' a loud alarm from his phone cut him short.

She frowned. 'What's that?'

'A reminder. We're going to be late for the munch.'

Karen turned aside. 'I don't think I want to go any more.'

'Of course you do. If I say so . . .'

No. Jesus, Dan, don't do that. Don't play the Dom card now. We were nearly there.

'I'd rather talk some more,' she murmured. 'I think there's a lot we should discuss.'

'Come on now . . .' Dan stalked closer, running his fingers around the waistband of his boxers as he advanced. Karen experienced a brief stab of satisfaction as she realised that instead of turning her on, the sight only irritated her. She backed off, hands raised.

'I need to clean my teeth.' She fled the bedroom to lock herself in the bathroom. As she spun the tap she hoped the sound of splashing water would block the roar of her pulse in her ears.

An hour later Karen sat in the front seat of Dan's grubby car, wearing tight black jeans and a purple vest. Her matching collar with the silver bell jangled every time the car took a speed bump. The tingle of the little instrument served as a constant audio cue.

She glanced right. 'I've never done one of these before. What's it like?'

Dan frowned at the road. 'Mostly a bunch of people eating homemade cakes and drinking cider. I doubt this group will be any different.'

'Any play?'

'No, it's in a pub, remember? You're wearing the collar because it's a quick and easy way of giving over the gist of our relationship. And also to let folk know you're taken.'

Taken. Like a seat at the cinema. Or a book off a shelf.

'Dan, I think we need—'

'We're here!' His excited voice cut across hers.

She looked up in time to see the car swing into a parking bay beside a beat up old Prius. 'Looks normal.'

'It *is* normal. Just a pub, remember?' He got out and waited for her to do the same before locking the doors. Then he set off, his hand trailing behind him, fingers twitching.

Karen caught up and grabbed his hand. 'Dan, wait. Can we talk for a second?'

'What?' He wasn't even looking, all ready waving at a small, sandy haired man in a rugby shirt. She recognised the face as one from Kink4Life. 'What's wrong?'

'I need you to stop so we can talk. We need to talk about subs. And you. And me.'

'Can't we do that inside? It's cold.'

'But—' she broke off with a yelp as two hands closed over her eyes, cutting out the car park and plunging her into darkness.

'Guess who?' a voice hissed in her ear.

To one side, she heard Dan laughing, followed by another giggle she knew very well. 'Denise?'

'There's my little kitten!' The hands vanished.

Karen whirled round. There stood Denise, a tall, broad figure with long, blond hair. He smiled, but then his gaze slid passed her to Dan. His eyes widened. 'What the hell happened to you?'

Despite their joined efforts with concealer, Dan's bruise was very much visible. He touched the area with the tip of his fingers. 'Long story.'

'Isn't this where you say 'you should see the other guy'?'

'Not this guy. Trust me, long, *long* story.'

Though Denise seemed unconvinced, he looked away from Dan and returned his attention to Karen. 'Kaz . . . come on, sweetheart, lay it on me.'

She looked again. Took in the simple blue skirt, just low enough on the hips to show a flash of flesh. Above it, a wrap-around blouse with short sleeves matched the floral pattern on a pair of two-inch heels.

'I didn't think you Dressed outside clubs.'

Denise waved a perfectly manicured hand. 'This munch is a safe, comfortable place. No one is going to judge me here. Besides, don't I look pretty in heels?'

Karen laughed. 'Business suits do nothing for you.'

'Exactly. Hug me, all ready.'

'It's good to see you,' said Karen, leaning in to kiss his powdered cheek.

He snorted and pulled her close, wrapping both arms around her in a big, strong hug. 'There. You okay, sweetheart?'

She gazed into his face, then at Dan who kept glancing towards the pub. 'I'm fine,' she murmured.

'Another 'long story'?'

She nodded, hoping her smile appeared more positive than she felt.

The conversation with Dan would have to wait.

'Fine. I'll leave it for now.' Denise threaded his arm through hers and towed her along. 'So, I hear you're meeting a new sub for the Library?'

'Maybe. If she shows up.'

'Don't be disappointed if she doesn't. It's daunting, meeting potential play partners for the first time.'

Arm in arm, they followed Dan into the pub. When he paused, searching the room, Denise tapped his shoulder.

'We're upstairs, sweetheart. I only came down to get my phone from the car. Henrietta's up there saving me a seat. Should be plenty of room for you two.'

'Thanks.' Dan darted up the stairs.

'Keen isn't he?' Denise bit his lip.

You have no idea.

/\ *

Upstairs greatly resembled the lower portion of the pub except for a few minor differences. The presence of fellow kinksters was obvious. Men and women wearing collars. Tattoos of the triskelion or the kajira. Subtle, but there for those who knew how to look.

Some of those gathered spared her only a glance before looking away again. Others paused long enough to give her a once-over, their gaze usually coming to rest on her collar. One look lasted longer than the others, an appreciative sweep from her head to her toes and back again. It ended on her face.

He was tall, with skin darker than her own, big kind eyes and a full head of dreadlocks.

For a horrible, heart-stopping moment she thought Robert had come to find her, but the stranger's ready smile made clear it was no one she knew.

He nodded and raised his glass to her, pushing a pair of narrow, wire-framed glasses up his nose and closer to his eyes.

Definitely not Robert. Wow.

She allowed herself a small smile in return.

Then Henrietta cut across her view, his usual brunet wig swapped for a vibrant red bob with an under flick.

'Good to see you, Karen.' As ever, he spoke in a near whisper, but Karen knew what to do by now. She pulled him close for a hug.

'Hey, that DVD you loaned us was *amazing!*'

When he pulled back, Henrietta wore a look she'd never seen before. Rather than timid and shy, he actually looked *playful.* 'That's just one of the collection. Wait until you see what I've brought with me.'

Grinning, Karen put out her hand and allowed him to tow her towards the bar.

DAN

Dan sipped his beer and ran a finger around the rim of the glass. 'Who's the guy with the dreadlocks?'

Swivelling in his seat, Denise followed his gaze over the bodies pressed shoulder to shoulder in the narrow bar. 'No idea. Why?'

'He keeps looking at Karen.'

'Maybe he is. Maybe he likes the look of her. Maybe he wants to talk to her. So what?'

'She's mine,' Dan growled. 'He shouldn't look at her that way.'

Denise flicked his hair. 'Pee on her then. Would that make you feel better?'

'You're no help,' he muttered.

'I am when you need it, but you're being silly. So a cute, young man is staring at your sub. Has she spoken to him? Has she given him another glance? Has she given any indication that she even knows he's there?'

'You think he's cute?'

'Daniel . . . '

'Fine, she hasn't.'

'Then stop worrying about it. Instead, make a decision about what *you* plan to do.'

'I can't. I don't *know* what to do. What would *you* do?' He hated to ask, it made his jaw ache, but there was no other choice. He *needed* advice and there was no one to ask but the grinning transvestite with the ruby lipstick.

Denise gave him a steady look from beneath the strands of his fringe. His eyes sparkled with mirth and as his mouth opened, Dan knew what was about to fall out of it.

'If you crack another joke, I'll punch you.'

'Like you did yourself?'

'I'm serious! You helped me before—whether you meant to or not—I'm just asking you to do that again. And don't call me 'sweetheart,' I can't handle it.'

'Well sweet—Dan, if you sure don't know how to beg for help.'

'I'm not begging. We're friends, aren't we? I need a friend to tell me what to do.'

'I thought you were the one in charge.'

'I am. And it's fucking hard. I need a break.'

Denise raised his hands as though that explained everything. 'Then isn't this perfect? Have a break, let Karen do her Domme thing and you can relax and enjoy it.'

'I don't know if I can.'

'What is it you're afraid of, Dan? This isn't about her taking your place.'

'It was never about that.' The words came out rougher than he intended but he couldn't help it. Then Dan looked at his friend again and realised he couldn't possibly know the truth. Not when he'd never admitted it, not even to himself. He focused on the amber liquid within his glass. 'She thinks I don't understand, but I do. Karen doesn't want to top *me*, that's not her game. She wants to top someone else.'

'You top other women.'

'That's different.' Even as the words left his mouth he winced.

Hypocritical or what?

'I don't want to *be* with other women. I like having them around. But Karen . . .'

'What about her?'

He toyed with the glass again, collecting condensation on the tip of his finger. A cool drop slid across the back of his hand and soaked into the cuff of his shirt. 'What if she finds someone she likes more?'

'What if?'

Dan glared. 'Aren't you supposed to tell me that won't ever happen?'

'Why? Lies won't help you, sweetheart.'

'Denise!'

'Well, they won't. She may find someone else, but it *is* unlikely. She loves you. Any idiot can see that.'

Some of the irritation began to ease. 'What if she likes topping more than being a sub?'

'Then you've got a Switch on your hands. Best of both worlds, if you ask me.'

'But . . .'

'What, Dan? What are you trying to say?'

'What if she doesn't want to be a sub any more?'

Denise snorted into his diet coke. 'You think she'll *grow out* of her need to submit?'

With it put like that, Dan felt silly. A flush of heat crept up the inside of his collar. 'You don't need to laugh at me.'

'I do. Because you're blind. Sweetheart, you're as blind as the sun is warm and it gives me great joy to lift the blindfold.'

'What the hell are you talking about?'

'Karen submits because she wants to. She *needs* it to balance the control she has everywhere else. I've not known her as long as you have, but surely you can see that. It rounds her off. Unless other parts of her personality change, I don't see how the submission is going to change.'

'But what about me?' He glanced passed Denise's shoulder to where Karen sat chatting to Henrietta. Her eyes were lively and bright, her features animated as she pointed to the stack of DVDs piled on the table between them. She tapped one and followed the blurb on the back with the tip of her finger. Her free hand unconsciously stroked the bell dangling from her collar. He could hear the faint tinkle over the general bustle of chatter and clanking glasses.

'What if she doesn't want to submit to *me* any more? What if she finds a Dom that does a better job?'

'How? Is she asking for another Dom?'

'No.'

'Then you're getting stressed and panicked over nothing. She doesn't want another dominant, she wants to *be* dominant. And she wants to dominate someone else which means your dynamic is safe.'

Dan tightened his grip on his glass. He still wasn't explaining very well. 'Not if she brings in another man. It's competition.'

'There *is* no competition.' Denise laid a hand on his knee. 'She loves you. If you turned to her now and said you didn't want to be her Dom any more, she would still love you. She wants *you*. The fact that you top her just makes it better. You're the complete package and unless she gives you some sign that she's interested in someone else, you'd better calm down and relax.'

It should have made him feel better. The facts—for facts they were—should have brought calm and peace to Dan's mind. But as he looked again at the stranger across the room and found him staring at Karen, he just felt worse.

'Thanks.' He stood and pointed to the table of empty glasses. 'Want another?'

'No, ta. This will last me.'

Before Dan could move towards the bar he felt his phone hum in his pocket. Denise gave him a brief nod and turned to join Henrietta's conversation with Karen, so Dan returned to his seat to answer it. 'Hello?'

'Hey, mate, only me. How's your face?'

The sound of Pete's voice lit a spark in Dan's mind. He tightened his grip on the phone, thinking hard while staring at the far wall. The idea came quickly. Almost fully formed in the back of his mind. He grinned.

Why didn't I think of this before? It's perfect.

'Fine. How's your arm?'

'Not bad. He may be tall, but he doesn't weigh all that much. It didn't take much to chuck him out. Is Karen okay?'

'Just shaken. And pissed off.' He thought again of her dark expression as she recounted her father's actions. So cold. So angry.

Pete laughed. 'I wouldn't want to be that guy right now. Is he really her dad?'

The memory still stung, but Dan hid it as best he could. 'Yes. Crazy but true.'

Pete took a deep breath. 'Listen, about last night, I'm so sorry. I wasn't thinking. I was drunk too. I didn't mean to cause trouble—and Karen—'

'Karen is fine,' he cut in.

'Really?'

'Yes. We talked about it this morning. You're an idiot and you never should have done it, but she'd rather forget it ever happened.'

'Wow. Okay. I guess if she says she's fine . . .'

'Water under the bridge. Listen, can I ask you something?'

Life and enthusiasm returned to Pete's voice. 'Sure, anything.'

Dan paused, chewing his bottom lip. He had to ask now. Straight away before he could lose his nerve. 'I need a favour.' Silence. 'Pete?'

'Yeah, I'm here. I just . . . lately your questions or favours get me in a shit load of trouble.'

'Not this time. This you'll like.'

'This? And what's 'this'?'

Dan fiddled with the hem of his shirt, tugging on a loose thread until it snapped. 'I want you to join me and Karen tonight. Just for a little while. Let her boss you around a bit. You know, like I do to her.'

More silence. This time Dan couldn't even hear breathing from the other end. He felt a stab of panic. 'Hello? Pete?' Nothing. He checked the phone. Frowned when he saw the call was still connected. 'Pete, you need to say something. Are you there?'

'You've cleared this with Karen?' His voice was small. Child-like.

'Yes. She wants a male sub to join the Library.'

'Like those other girls? No way.'

'Don't worry. No one will be flogging or spanking you. She wants to mess around a bit. You know, blindfolds, handcuffs, feathers. Ann Summers sort of stuff. Nothing hard core.'

'Right. And she wants me?'

'Better you than some creep off the Internet. Besides, you're a friend. We both know where we stand with you.'

'I'm not sure. After last night—'

Dan scoffed. 'Don't worry about last night. I told you, it's sorted. In fact, don't even mention it again. And you'll be doing us both a favour. This is what she wants.'

'Really?'

He sighed. 'To my eternal confusion, yes.'

Just talking to Pete calmed him. The nagging worries of earlier faded in the face of planning what he would need.

She can get it out of her system and it will be over. Much better with Pete than some creep who just wants to get into her knickers.

'I don't know what to say,' mumbled Pete.

'Say you'll do it. Trust me, you'll have a great time. You told me a few weeks back you wanted to try some of this 'kinky shit.' And you were whining about me sharing. Now you can see for yourself.'

'Okay.' A little quiver filled Pete's voice as he spoke. Dan knew his friend well enough to recognise excitement. 'I'll do it. What do I need? Condoms?'

'No. And don't get any ideas. Just because we're playing doesn't mean there will be sex. We're just scratching an itch for Karen, understand?'

'Right.'

'Good. Come to our place at eight.'

'I will. Thanks mate. And thanks for clearing up that business last night too. I don't know what you said but if she's forgiven me it must have been good.'

'Don't mention it. I'll see you later.'

He hung up, already planning the evening ahead.

Getting Karen all fired up was the most fun of any play session, then leaving her wanting while other members of the Library played. It heightened everything until both of them wanted nothing more than to explode in orgasmic bliss. Reaching that point and then telling her what he had in store would be perfect.

He could almost see the pleasure in her eyes.

She smiled at him from across the bar. He waved back, then a twinge from stomach level reminded him of his need for the bathroom. He used the facilities quickly, still tweaking his plans. By the time he returned to the bar, the plan was set in his mind. All he had to do was surprise Karen with his plan after dinner. She would be so excited.

The thought of it made him groan aloud.

On the way back he brushed passed the man with long hair like Robert's. Broad shouldered and slim at the waist, he looked more like a footballer than anyone Dan associated with kink.

The man smiled as he went by, a shy half grin. Dan stiffened, preparing to warn him off, but the man merely nodded. He did the same, now keen to reach the others and put his arm around Karen's shoulders.

The stranger made a small sound, as if he meant to speak, but Henrietta chose that moment to grab Dan's arm. 'Dan! You really must pick one of these DVDs.'

'Sure. One sec.' He paused, but a glance at the stranger showed he had already returned to a previous conversation. The moment passed.

KAREN

Karen tapped Dan on the shoulder. 'Another beer? Or something softer?'

'Softer. I'm driving, remember?' He handed her a curled up twenty.

At the bar, after ordering two glasses of lemonade, she looked back at the cluster of kinksters chatting.

So many of them . . . from so many different backgrounds.

Max the accountant. Diane the secondary school teacher. Cheryl the prison officer. Sith the barrister in training.

As if to think his name was a summons, Sith approached, his dreadlocks pulled down over one shoulder. By now accustomed to his look and assured he was nothing like Robert, Karen smiled as he stopped beside her. 'Hey, it's Sith, right?'

He propped an elbow on the bar. 'Actually it's Sithembile.'

'Sithembile. What a mouthful.'

'Most people stick with Sith.'

'Then I will too. Sorry we've not had a chance to talk. It's really busy. Is that normal?'

'No clue. I've only been to this munch once before.'

'Really? You have the look of a veteran about you.'

'Is that right?' He leaned closer, flashing a smile that was all white teeth and dimples. 'I could say the same for you. You look pretty comfortable hugging people, talking about dirty DVDs and tinkling that little bell.'

Karen tossed her head, hard enough to make said bell give a jaunty ring. 'You like it?'

'Very much.' He chuckled, warm sound, like melted butter run through chocolate.

The appearance of two lemonade glasses saved Karen the need to answer. Not that she could have said anything that made sense. Her tongue stuck in her mouth, thick and awkward behind her teeth. A prickle of heat filled her face. She longed to touch the cool glasses against her cheeks and forehead. Instead, she cleared her throat. 'Dan bought it for me. I like purple.'

'Dan.' Sith's smile deepened. He turned and pointed. Is that Mr Salt'N'Pepper over there?'

Why is everyone obsessed with Dan's hair?

She nodded. 'That's right.'

'He's cute.'

Karen paused in her gazing at Dan to reassess Sith. His smile remained in place. Teasing. Gentle. 'I'm sorry, what?'

'Oh—is that not allowed? Like I said, I'm new; I don't know if I'm allowed to say that, when he's clearly yours.'

Karen looked at him again. And again. She took a hasty swallow from her lemonade. 'Um . . . no, no, it's fine. I just didn't think you—I mean, you don't look like—what am I saying, here?'

He cocked an eyebrow. 'You mean I don't look like a gay guy?'

Shit.

'That's not what I mean.' She frowned. 'Okay, it is. But you don't.'

'What does a gay guy look like?'

'. . . I don't know.'

'Well, I'm not gay. I *do* like men, but not gay. Pansexual.'

'And what the hell does that mean?'

He chuckled. It was a soft, self depreciating sound and, despite her confusion, Karen found her body warming in places other than her face.

'It means I'm attracted to all genders and sexual identities.'

'You mean bisexual?'

'No.' His voice hardened. '*Pan*sexual. Bisexuals are attracted to males and females while I—or should I say those who identify as pansexual—are attracted to non binary genders too.'

She raised her hands in mock-surrender. 'I don't know what most of that means. Sorry if I offended you.'

'You didn't offend me, I just want to be clear. There's often confusion so I try to make it easy to understand.' He leaned forward. 'I'd be happy to go through it with you in more detail.'

Karen tightened her grip on the lemonade. She didn't remember picking them up, but holding the cool, moist glass offered some defence against the warmth billowing through the rest of her body.

Sith stood close, his hip almost touching hers. He stooped to look at her, blocking her view of anything beyond his shoulder. His hair swayed as he shifted his weight, brushing close enough to smell. Lemon and something else . . . possibly ginger.

She licked her lips. 'That's very kind. Maybe later, though.'

Sensing her mood, Sith leaned away. He took his sweet smelling hair with him and wrapped his own slender fingers around his glass of coke. 'Find me on Kink4Life. I assume you're there since everyone else seems to be? I'm *Black Angelus*. And before you ask, the picture *isn't* my usual one. It's normally my face. Promise.'

The subject change returned Karen a little of her confidence. She grinned. 'What *is* your picture?'

'You'll laugh.'

'Probably. Go on; spill it.'

He bit his lip.

'Aaaah, you've got a dick-pic as your profile picture, haven't you?' Karen laughed. 'God, you're not one of *those* guys, are you?' She walked back to the table. Someone had taken her chair, so she left Dan his drink and found an empty seat nearby.

Sith dragged a hand through his hair. He appeared truly mortified as he trotted after her. 'It was a dare! Which I lost. It stays for two more weeks then it's back to normal, I swear.' He perched on a stool next to her. 'And what do you mean 'those guys?''

'Dick-pic guys?' She thumped her glass on the table. 'The arrogant idiots who think they're impressive just because they have a long cock. The guys who think 'this is all those *lay-deehs* want to see, so I'll just leave it here to fuel their fantasies.''

'Oh, *those* guys. No, I'm not one of those. My cock is all about girth.' Sith winked and adjusted his glasses with a playful waggle of his eyebrows.

Karen snorted into her lemonade. 'You have an answer for everything, don't you?'

'I hope so. What kind of barrister would I be if I didn't?'

'What's your *actual* picture?'

'You'll laugh.' He lowered his head.

'You said that before. Was it another dick-pic?'

'No . . . it's me in a strapedo-tie.'

Further waves of warmth swirled through Karen's body. She shifted on her stool and crossed her legs. 'I sense there's more to this.'

He frowned. 'Fine, a strapedo-tie and a ball gag.'

'And?'

'Strapedo-tie, ball gag and nipple clamps.'

She gave him a pointed stare.

'And a chastity device.' Sith's voice dropped to a barely audible whisper.

'There, that wasn't so bad, was it?' Karen patted him on the knee. 'And why would I laugh? Sounds like fun.'

Sith's head snapped up. His eyes glimmered with hope. 'Really?'

'Why not?'

'Because I spend a lot of time domming. It's nice—of course it is, you'd know—but every once in a while I'd like to change it up. You know . . . feel the lash every now and then.'

'What do you mean, 'I'd know'?'

'You're a Switch, right?' He looked her up and down.

Karen touched her cheek. 'What makes you say that?'

'Because you are. You *are* a switch?'

'No.'

'For real?'

She forced a chuckle. 'Do I really give off the vibe?'

'The 'I'll spank you if you cross me' vibe? Yes, you do.'

'Wow.' Her cheeks warmed and though she fought it, she failed to resist the little rush of pleasure. 'Thanks. I think.'

'It's a compliment. Promise.'

'I'll take your word for it. So that's what you want? When you talk about 'feeling the lash'?'

He shrugged. 'I like to be tied up. Used. Even humiliated, sometimes. It's a rush. But you know about that part.'

Karen's breath caught in her throat. She risked a glance at Dan, but he was too absorbed in his conversation with Denise to notice. 'I love it.'

Sith's expression became mild. Questioning. 'You look confused.'

She shook her head. 'It's nothing to do with you. You're great—I mean this is great. Ugh.' She bit her lip. 'Sorry, I'm usually more coherent than a teenager.'

'Pity.'

This time Karen couldn't hide her embarrassment. She took another slurp of lemonade. Choked. She slammed a fist against her chest.

'You okay?'

'Yes,' she muttered, flicking sticky liquid off her fingers. 'If you don't count embarrassed and tongue-tied.'

'Don't worry, I won't tell anyone. Your spankilious street cred is safe with me.'

More laughter. This time real and loud enough to draw curious glances. 'Oh, good. I'd hate to lose spanking credability with the Warhammer 40k crowd.'

Sith grinned. 'You forgot Dungeons and Dragons. And the Marvel movies.'

'Yes . . . the *real* loves of the kinky munch crowd. That and arranging an illicit hookup.'

'Is that what we're doing? Hooking up?'

She paused, staring out over his head at the milling crowds. 'I don't know. Do you want to?'

His gaze flicked over her shoulder toward Dan. Then back again. Slowly up and down her body before returning to her eyes. 'Yes.'

Karen's face burned. She felt sure her skin might catch fire at any moment.

'You don't have to say anything.' He touched her knee. It was a tiny, feather-light touch, but she felt it through her entire body. 'I don't want to be pushy or weird, but I like you. You're funny, smart and friendly. Your Dom is hot too. I haven't spoken to him yet, or else I'm sure I'd have something more intelligent to say.'

'You think he's hot?'

'Don't you?'

She glanced over her shoulder.

Dan's face was fixed in an expression of deep concentration. He leaned forward, listening to Denise as he and a woman she didn't know explained the merits of cricket over football. When they finished, Dan shook his head and began his rebuttal.

His hands moved as much as his mouth, giving energetic weight to his verbal argument. A lock of dark hair, streaked with grey, flopped down into his eyes. He flicked it impatiently away. When it fell back again a moment later, he held it in place with his left hand, causing the muscles in his bicep to bunch against his shirt.

Karen blew a deep breath through her lips. 'He's the sexiest man I've ever known. The strongest, the kindest, the sweetest, the most loving.' She touched her bell, then fingered the links of the slave band across the back of her hand.

'Did he get you that?' Sith touched the bracelet, tracing one of the chains with his index finger.

'It's my Collar.' She said it carefully, watching his face to see if he understood the emphasis.

He immediately jerked his hand back. 'Sorry, I didn't realise.'

'No, it's fine. Not the traditional Collar, right?'

'I've never seen anything like it.'

'They're around, but this is a custom design.' She didn't try to keep the pride from her voice. 'He wanted three rings to signify the three different pillars of our relationship. Honesty, trust and friendship.'

Sith stroked his jaw. 'That's deep. How long have you guys been together?'

'Two years.'

'And you still have playmates?'

'You have no idea.' Karen grinned, as she tried to decide how much to share. 'We have an arrangement called a Slave Library. Basically, Dan's building a harem.'

Sith's eyes grew round with delight. 'Wow.'

'There's only three of us so far, but he's always looking to expand. And one of the other girls is going mono soon.'

'Other girls? Just girls?' Some of the interest died from his eyes. He toyed with the hem of his shirt.

Only after a moment did Karen understand why. 'Sorry, I don't know what I was thinking. Dan is purely straight.'

'Damn. Fair enough. But what about *your* Library?'

'I don't have one. Is it really so hard to believe I'm just a sub?'

He turned up his nose with a teasing snort. 'Don't believe you.'

'We've talked about it,' she murmured. 'But he won't even consider the idea of adding men to the Library. He says the thought makes him uncomfortable.'

'So no men for Dan . . . but women don't make *you* uncomfortable?'

'I'm bisexual, I love women. They're so freaking sexy. But sometimes I want—never mind.'

'What?'

'I shouldn't have said anything. Don't worry about it.'

Sith gave her a shrewd look. 'Sore spot? Sorry, but your Dom sounds like he's getting a great deal. A dream come true for most guys. What about you?'

'I get plenty of fun. He takes good care of me.'

'Does he?'

The question hung in the air, an invisible, delicate bubble. Karen longed to pop it with a joke, or blow it away with confident nonchalance, anything to save her from dwelling on the answer. But the words lingered and the longer she remained silent, the heavier and bigger they became.

'Of course.' Another slurp of lemonade gave her a moment to think. 'He's always thinking of me. I get everything I need when I submit. Dan knows what makes me tick.'

'He knows but doesn't provide, from the sound of it.'

She bristled. Though it simultaneously surprised her, it comforted Karen to know that she still felt protective of Dan and her relationship with him.

Firm and deliberate, she set her glass on the table and leaned back. 'Listen, Sith, I know you mean well, but this is really none of your—' She broke off, staring at the door from the stairs as a new figure stepped into view.

He was familiar, in an eerie way. Skinny. Simple, boring clothes and shoes, but his long white hair swept out from his face like a wild fan to match the whiskers around his jaw and chin.

When he looked up, Karen grunted as though punched in the gut.

Holy fucking fuck.

She stood, then immediately dropped to a crouch behind a cluster of other kinksters.

'Karen?' Sith peered at her, his expression borderline stony. 'Sorry if I offended you, but I think you should be able to—'

'Shut up,' she hissed.

Hurt blossomed in Sith's eyes. Karen ignored it, watching the familiar figure.

Oh my god, it can't be. It is. It is!

'Karen—'

'Don't say my name!' She stood, darted away from Sith and plunged her hand through Dan's conversation. He gave a cry of alarm as she heaved on his shirt collar. 'We need to leave,' she snapped.

'Kaz, what—'

'Your dad is here!'

'What? No, he's having brunch with Mum.'

Karen pointed.

Dan choked. Colour drained from his face. He gave a little moan, dropping low behind Henrietta's back. 'Fuck!'

'I know. Let's just go. He hasn't seen us yet. We can use the back way.' She straightened and angled herself towards the opposite set of steps.

Sith stepped across her path. 'Karen, please don't go. Sorry if I said something out of line, but you don't need to leave. Aren't you overreacting?'

In the corner of her eye, Julian broke away from the greeters near the door and wandered over. He appeared comfortable, calm. Not at all like a man walking into a meeting he didn't want to be part of. When he eventually grinned and waved at someone near the back, Karen knew the grim, slightly nauseating truth. Her insides squirmed. Dan's grip on her hand tightened.

'Sith, I'm sorry. I can't explain now, but I have to go.'

He caught her arm. She snatched it back.

'Karen, please!' he cried.

Dan was already there, shouldering his way between them without a backward glance.

Sith actually stumbled, forced to steady himself on the back of his stool. 'Karen . . .'

She backed off, hands raised. 'I've got to go. I'm sorry.' With that, she followed Dan, forcing her way through the press of bodies to reach the rear stairs.

DAN

Dan's pulse hammered the back of his throat so hard he could almost taste it. Coat dangling from one arm, fingers still wrapped around his lemonade glass, he reached the back the bar and paused.

On the other side of the room, greeting kinksters like long-lost friends, Julian grinned and shook hands. A second later he sat close to Henrietta and held out his hand. His lips formed the word 'Hi.'

Startled by Dan's sudden exit, Denise swivelled to face him, his expression one of raw confusion. He pointed.

Dan stopped struggling into his coat long enough to wave his arms frantically, mouthing 'NO!' with big, exaggerated motions of his mouth.

Denise held up his hands in question.

'Father,' he mouthed back, begging the other man to understand. 'He's my father.'

Denise widened his eyes and pointed to Julian.

'Yes!'

Jesus, this is the last thing I need. He can't see me here.

He laughed. From across the room, Dan heard Denise's guffaw of laugher and longed to punch something. He didn't, instead pressing his hands together to mime begging. 'Please, don't.'

A quick thumbs up and shake of the head from the other man allowed Dan to release the breath he'd been holding. 'Thank you.'

The look on Denise's face said he'd pay for it later, but in that moment, Dan could think of nothing other than remaining unseen.

Karen stood beside him, her face slack with worry. 'Did he see us?'

'I don't think so.'

'What the hell is he doing here?'

Dan clenched his fists. 'Meeting other kinksters from the look of it. Not for the first time either. Shit.'

'Did you know?'

'Of course not! Do you think I would have brought you here if I knew he was coming?'

'I was just asking,' she shot back.

Every scrap of sense he possessed urged him to leave. To walk away and pretend he hadn't seen a thing. But another part, a terribly curious part, with no sense of self-preservation, longed to find out more.

'Maybe they're just old friends and he spotted them at the bar.' Karen's voice was more hopeful than her expression.

Dan grunted. 'Old friends? Is that why he's holding a dildo the size of a cucumber?' As he said it the bile rose in his throat. He clutched his stomach, but the spasm passed quickly. As Julian brandished a long green box, with a plastic window showing a black, heavily veined dildo, Dan couldn't help but wonder if he'd fallen headlong into a bizarre nightmare.

I'm still in bed. This is a dream from when Robert punched me. I'll wake up in a minute, in bed, with a massive bruise and a hangover.

To speed up the process, he pinched his arm. The pain drew a yelp from his lips. 'Oh, good God,' he moaned. 'Dad's a kinkster.'

'Dan, let's go.' Karen tugged his arm. 'Why are you standing there?'

'I can't believe it. I need to see.'

'No, you don't. You need to get out of here and keep your mind clean of any weird stuff your dad might be getting up to with those kinky fuckers we know and love.'

He faced her. 'Weird? Is that what *we* are? Is that what *we* do?'

She hesitated. 'No. But come on, Dan. It's your *dad*. Do you really want to see that? There are some things you don't share with your parents.'

She was right, but Dan couldn't take his eyes off the familiar form of his father sitting to one side of Denise and Henrietta.

'Mum isn't here,' he said at last.

Karen rolled her eyes. 'Good. At least if Julian sees you he won't rip you a new ear hole talking about it. But Maxine?'

'Kaz, Mum's not here.' He narrowed his eyes at his father's profile.

'Yes, I got that.'

'That means Dad is here *without her*.' He watched Karen open her mouth to speak, then snap it shut again.

'Oh . . . oh! But he wouldn't—not your mum. Not Maxine, no way.'

'I can't see Mum going for any of this stuff.'

Karen gripped his arm. 'But Julian wouldn't cheat on her. He loves her, despite the crazy—maybe *because* of the crazy—but he'd never cheat on her.'

He shook her loose and clutched the door frame. 'Your dad cheated on Charlaine.'

Her lips tightened. 'Robert is an arsehole. If he hadn't got Mum pregnant, he would never have stuck around long enough to cheat on her. Your dad is different, trust me, This isn't the same.'

'Then where is she?' He craned his neck, standing on tip toes to see over the milling crowd. 'Where's Mum?'

'I don't know.'

He'd heard enough. Thought enough. Turning away he thundered down the stairs and through the back rooms of the pub. Only when the doors slammed behind him, did he hear Karen's bell jangling as she dashed to keep up.

The car groaned as he jerked the doors open and the silence within warred with the battle raging in his head.

Karen clambered in beside him and placed her hand on his knee. 'What can I do?' Her voice was gentle. Hushed. The same voice one used in funeral homes or care centres for the elderly.

'I don't know.'

'Maybe we should go home?'

'Yeah.' He started the car, the ache from his knotted jaw crawling up the side of his skull. 'Let's do that.'

Dan paced the living room, a beer in one hand, his mobile in the other. Karen watched him from the sofa, her face a curious mix of pain and concern. 'What do you mean you don't know?' he snarled into the mouthpiece.

From the other end of the phone, Maxine gave a small huff of impatience. 'I don't know how else to say it, darling. I don't know where he is. I felt terribly ill after the party, so I stayed here. I think he went shopping.'

'Dad? Shopping? Are we talking about the same man?'

'Of course, Daniel. Do stop being silly. Now tell me what this is all about.'

'It's fine.' He tangled his fingers in his hair.

'Something must be wrong. You're clearly terribly upset. I know, I'll come over—'

'No!' He thumped the bottle against the fireplace. 'Sorry. Don't let me disturb your rest.'

'It's no trouble, darling. It's my job to look after you.'

Dan gritted his teeth. 'No, it isn't.'

'But I want to. Is Karen there? Does *she* know why you're so upset?' An accusatory barb crept into her voice.

He cut a glance at his girlfriend and saw her sneak her laptop from beneath the TV. 'She's fine,' he murmured. 'She's doing everything she needs to.'

'If you're certain. When your father returns, I'll tell him you were asking for him. Would that make you feel better?'

'No, don't worry about it. I'll talk to you later.'

'Bye, darling.' She made soft kissing noises.

Dan hung up. Burying his face in his hands, he flopped on to the sofa beside Karen, hard enough to make her bells chime. 'You can take that off now, you know.'

She stroked it, barely lifting her gaze from the laptop screen. 'I like wearing it.'

That made him smile. 'I like seeing you wearing it. Is that *Kink4Life*?'

'Yep. I thought I'd check the comments from the munch.'

He nodded, only half listening. His head whirled through dozens of questions, none of which he had the answers to.

He thought again of his father, struggling to pin point exactly what it was about the idea that made him so uncomfortable.

Was it that his dad was interested in kink at all? Or that they *both* were? That his mother had no idea what was going on? Did he really think his father was a cheater?

He picked up the phone again and dialled out.

It rang once before connecting. 'Daniel, my boy.'

He swallowed. 'Hey Dad. Can I talk to you? Is this a bad time?'

'Of course not. I'm in a cab on my way back to the hotel. What's the matter?'

'A cab? Where's Mum?'

'I left her in the room bemoaning her sore head. Apparently she hasn't felt so sickly since her student days.' He laughed. 'Did she ever tell you how much of a rebel she was when she was younger?'

Dan snorted. Though he had every intention of trying one of the cookies he'd managed to salvage from the night before, now was not the time. 'Only when trying to convince me not to do the same.' He raked a hand through his hair. 'What were you up to?'

Julian hesitated. 'I stopped to pick up some odds and sods for your mother, then had a drink at the pub. Just one or two while the cricket was playing.'

In his mind's eye, Dan saw a cricket match playing on the big screen mounted on a wall in a far corner of the pub. He licked his lips. 'See anyone you know?'

'As a matter of fact, yes. Odd—it's a long time since I socialised in this city—but I saw a few faces I recognised.'

'Where from?'

'The working men's club back in Ely. Dan, are you okay? You sound peculiar.'

'I'm fine.' His grip tightened on the phone. Once more he paced the length of the room.

'What did you want to talk about? Surely not how I spent my day.'

Dan flexed his fingers, then forced them to loosen. The knot of stiffness in his jaw pulled tight. 'Actually, I wanted to talk about Robert.'

'Karen's father?'

'Yes. He cheated on Charlaine. Lots of times. He still does from what I can tell.'

Silence from the other end.

'Dad?'

'Yes, I'm here, my boy. Just confused. You want to talk to me about Karen's dad's marital issues?'

'That's right. I want to know what you think.'

'Well,' he stretched the word. 'If Charlaine is anything at all like Karen in her looks, then I'd say this Robert character is a special kind of idiot. I didn't get a good look at her last night before things got overexcited. A shame as I would have liked to talk to her. How's your face by the way?'

'What?'

'That punch. Did you bruise?'

Dan touched his cheek. He barely remembered the pain with this new, all consuming distraction. 'I'm fine. We were talking about Robert?'

'Oh, yes. Well, I'd also say if Charlaine is anything like Karen personality-wise then he doesn't deserve her either.'

'But the cheating. What do you think of that?'

Julian's voice hardened. 'It takes a special kind of man to cheat on his wife. To break the vows he made before family, friends and God. A man like that doesn't deserve the love of a woman.'

'Really?' The sick feeling returned to Dan's gut. He swallowed it down.

'I know not all marriages last and that some relationships fold, but there's no reason why that can't be dealt with in a sensible, grown up manner. Sneaking around, lying, cheating—that's wrong. There's no excuse.'

Confusion and distress slowly hardened into anger. 'No, there isn't.'

A long pause followed. 'Is something happening between you and Karen?'

'Excuse me?'

'Sometimes you take a roundabout route like this to tell me about your problems. You used to do it when you were younger, all these *hypothetical* questions about this, that and the other when what you really wanted was advice. Are you asking for advice, my boy?'

'You mean, am I cheating on Karen?' He gnawed his lip until a hot burst of metallic fluid told him he was bleeding.

More silence.

'No, Dad. I'm *not* cheating on her. I never would. I don't have to. Our relationship doesn't work that way.'

'I've upset you. I'm sorry, but I don't know what to say. Unless you can be more open about what you're really trying to ask.' A hushed whisper cut across his voice. 'Sorry, I must pay this fine gentleman and get out of his car, but I need both hands. My hips aren't what they used to be.'

Dan sighed. 'It's okay. You've told me what I need to know.'

'Good. I hope so. I need to go.'

'Fine. Bye Dad.' He hung up without waiting for an answer.

At his side, Karen looked away from her laptop screen. She gazed at him for long, steady seconds. 'He's not cheating on Maxine.'

'I don't know what to believe.'

'You think he'd lie to you?'

'I don't know.' He sighed and shuffled across the sofa, curling his arm around her shoulder. He buried his nose in the space beneath her ear. 'I *do* know that I don't want to talk about it any more. I just want to sit with you and browse slaves for the Library.'

'I messaged Mandy to apologise.'

'Who?'

'The sub, Dan.' She gave him a playful shove. 'The one we went there to meet in the first place.'

It all seemed so long ago. A distant dream where life was normal and the kink scene, safe. 'Great. What did she say?'

'She didn't go. She chickened out as she got to the car park. Just turned around and drove away.'

'Wuss.'

'You do come on a bit strong sometimes, Spanx.'

The use of his online handle brought a smile to his lips. 'Do I?'

'Yes. All those pictures on your profile and the list of subs under your name.'

'Only three.'

'That's more than most people. Anyway, she wants to try again another time. She says she'll arrive early—wherever it is—and have a few drinks first.'

He nodded. 'Fine.' A glance at the laptop made him frown. 'That's not her, though. Who's *Black Angelus*?'

Karen cleared her throat. 'Someone I was talking to today.'

'Nice.'

The rest of the details attracted him just as much. Single. Submissive. Actively seeking playmates. Local.

Some of his anger and confusion began to ease away. 'Show me some of the pictures.'

Karen tapped and swiped at the trackpad. Seconds later a picture appeared. A naked back, broad across the shoulders which were the same dark colour as Karen's own skin. Dan couldn't help but lick his lips.

Very, very nice.

The next shot showed two feet in a spreader bar. Another, a close up of a deep purple nipple, pinched tight by a silver nipple clamp.

He grinned. 'Very nice. Let's see her face.'

Karen took a deep breath. 'It's not a woman.' She didn't look at him but continued sweeping through the photos.

The on screen nipple vanished, replaced by an image of a tall, stubbly man with dreadlocks. His eyes were closed, but his expression spoke volumes, as did his erect penis, jutting over the top of half lowered boxers. His arms were chained above his head, stretched far enough to make the muscles across his neck and shoulders bunch and cord. Sweat gleamed on his bare chest. A huge, red ball gag stretched his mouth.

His mouth.

Dan sat back. 'Oh.'

KAREN

Karen felt Dan stiffen beside her. His hand stopped massaging her shoulder.

I knew this was a bad idea.

He stared at the screen. A muscle pulsed in the side of his jaw.

Her chest tightened. *Say something. Please.*

'*Black Angelus.*' He made no attempt to hide the disapproving curl of his upper lip. 'What sort of name is that?'

Biting her tongue, she flicked to a more recent picture of Sith's back.

A grunt. 'Tattoos? Of course. How original.'

'You're upset,' she murmured. Her hands trembled on the lid of the laptop.

'No, I'm just surprised.' His voice didn't match the forced air of nonchalance. His hand bunched into a fist on her shoulder.

'I'm sorry,' she blurted. 'I shouldn't have brought him up— but we were talking about subs—he seems really nice.'

'You've spoken? When?'

'He was at the munch. I was talking to him when your dad showed up.' The moment the words left her mouth Karen knew it was the wrong thing to say.

Dan wrenched away from her, and paced the room. He retrieved his bottle from the fireplace and swigged. After a moment he pressed the rim to his lips and tipped it back, drinking, drinking and drinking some more until the contents were utterly spent. He burped.

'Dan—'

'What's he like?' he snapped. 'What does he do?'

'He's a barrister—in training.'

'Nice. Good for him. Bet he's loaded too.'

Karen snapped her lips shut over a cutting retort. After a quick breath she simply said, 'What does that have to do with anything?'

'Nothing. Just making small talk about our potential slave.' He spat the word as though it tasted bad.

'He's not a potential anything. We were just *talking*.'

'About BDSM?'

She rolled her eyes. 'It *was* a munch, Dan.'

'Did you happen to mention you're taken?'

'It's the first thing I said. I showed him my slave band.'

'And what did he think of that?'

'He liked the idea of the commitment. He said it was deep.'

''Deep.' Wow, cheers.' Dan raised the bottle again, giving a little snarl when he found it empty. 'Want another?'

'No, and neither should you. We're talking. Please don't run off while we're talking. You're upset and I need to know why.'

'I'm Master around here. Don't tell me what to do.'

Karen flinched. Something in her chest clenched tight, squeezing until she could barely breathe. Then anger barrelled in and flattened everything. She put the laptop on the sofa. Leapt up. 'Fuck you and your Master talk, that's not what we are right now.'

He glared at her. 'Of course it is. We're only a step away from 24/7.'

'No, we're not. Unless we're in scene, I'm 'Karen', you're 'Dan' and we talk to each other like adults. Get a fucking grip.'

He spun on his heel and stalked toward her. In that moment, his eyes blazed and the curls of his dark hair fell down over his forehead. Karen felt the energy building that told her she was about to enter a scene.

'Why don't I get a grip on you, Kaz? Why don't I show you who's in charge?' His voice dropped low and deep, rumbling at the back of his throat like a feral growl. He tossed his head to clear his eyes and breathed deep to swell his chest.

Her body responded instantly, nipples hardening beneath the fabric of her vest. She took a long step out of range. 'Don't do that. Don't hide behind 'Master' because you don't want to talk. You're pissed off and I don't submit to anybody when they're angry.'

He reached for her. Whether to grip her arm, cup her cheek or touch her throat, she never knew. Karen leapt on to the sofa, almost trampling her laptop to stay out of reach. She wasn't afraid, but she knew that any conversation she wanted to have would never happen if he managed to touch her.

'Stop it! What's wrong with you? Why won't you talk to me?'

Maybe the sight of her wobbling on the sofa cushions broke through his anger. Maybe it was the venom in her voice. Whatever it was, Dan stopped moving. His shoulders dropped and some of the tension oozed out of his body. 'I . . .'

'What, Dan? This is so . . . *not you*. You're not angry or violent . . . what is this about?' Her voice quivered, but she didn't care. The latent panic from even mentioning Sith left her weak in the knees. She licked her lips, trying to wet them but her tongue refused to cooperate.

Karen didn't get off the sofa, but sank into the cushions, pulling her knees up to her chest. When Dan tried to step closer, she leaned back and shot out one hand to keep him at bay.

Part of her wanted to scream and shout. The rest wanted to hide. Ignoring both, she opted to stay put. This conversation had to happen. Now.

'Stay right where you are. Talk. What the hell is wrong with you? Is this because of your dad?'

'Yes.' He ran a hand through his hair, holding the strands up off his forehead. 'No. I don't know.'

'Dan!'

'Fine, I'm pissed off. I have no idea what to do about Dad or how I feel. I'm just relieved he didn't see me at the pub and doubly relieved he didn't tell me straight out on the phone.'

'And Sith?'

'Who?'

She tapped the laptop.

'What the hell sort of name is Sith?'

'It's short for Sithembile.'

'Wow. So his parents couldn't do what yours did and give him a simple English name?'

Her mouth dropped open. 'That better be a joke. Robert is Jamaican. Mama is from Cornwall, you arsehole.'

'I know, I know, bad taste. Sorry. I'm teasing.'

'Fucking don't! We're talking.' Karen gazed at him. She tried to read his face, but his expressions were all over the place, flitting from anxious to angry, to distressed, to sad, to amused over and over. 'What is this about? One picture of a cute guy shouldn't send you into meltdown.'

'You think he's cute?'

'Dan!'

'Sorry.'

She toyed with the links of her slave band. 'I didn't ask for him to be your sub. *You* assumed. I wouldn't have mentioned him at all if you hadn't seen him on screen.' Karen looked at her fingers, stunned that such a small, yet truthful admission could make her feel so uncomfortable. 'In fact, I barely said anything before you went Jykell-Hyde on me. So what gives?'

He toyed with the edge of his sleeve. 'I don't know.'

'Then figure it out, because you're making me crazy.'

He glared. 'Fine. Why are you so desperate to bring a man into our relationship?'

'I'm not.' Determined to be the sensible one, Karen immediately told the truth. 'I've always wanted to see men in the Library but you told me back at Sugar Dust that it wasn't going to happen. I made peace with that. Hannah, Rebecca, Louise, Dani, any other girl you decide to bring along is fine by me so long as we stick to the rules we set at the start. No lies. No sneaking around. Full disclosure. The right to veto. I'm secure and happy with that.'

'Then why are you looking up *Black Angelus*?' That bite in his voice again. Tense shoulders. Narrowed eyes.

Another deep breath. 'Maybe I want to talk to him? Maybe I want to have *friends* in the kink scene?'

'What about Denise and Henrietta?'

She narrowed her eyes. 'What about them?'

'Be friends with them. At least they're not—' He glared at the floor.

Karen unfurled her legs. Stood. "They're not' what? A threat? Any sort of competition because they're gay and so obviously into each other that no one else pings on their radar?'

The moment she said it, she knew she'd struck truth.

Dan pressed his lips into a thin, grim line and jerked away. He stared at the blank eye of the TV and said nothing.

'Dan, look at me. I'm not saying another word until you look at me.'

Slowly, as if every inch was pain, he swivelled to face her.

She held up her left hand, showing off the slave band. 'Honesty. Trust. Friendship. That's everything special about you and me, right here on my wrist. You waited until Beth nearly tore us apart to give this to me, but it means as much to me now as it did then.'

'I thought you were going to leave me.'

'I was. Until you gave me this and told me in your own way that you love me. And I love *you*, Dan. I don't want anybody else, not the way I want you. You don't need to worry about Sith or anybody else *stealing* me away from you.'

He gave a tiny smile.

'He's more interested in you anyway.'

The smile died. 'Come again?'

'He thinks you're hot. I agree, so straight away we had a lot in common.' The joke fell flat on the air, like a frying pan to the face.

'He's gay too?'

'Pansexual.'

He raised his hands toward the ceiling in a 'why me' sort of gesture. 'Whatever the hell *that* means.'

'Dan, please, can't you just relax?'

'What about him? Does he know you 'just want more friends'?'

The pity she felt for his insecurities faded rapidly. 'Sith is cute. He's also new, shy and sweet. And *submissive*, Dan.' She clenched her fists, as if to steel herself, and rushed on. 'I know you trust me, but I don't *want* to dominate *you*. That's not our dynamic. It would feel wrong. Especially after all the horrible things Beth did to you while you were together. I need a lot more experience before I'd feel safe going anywhere near you with a whip or a paddle. I don't want to hurt you the way she did. But I *do* want to try. Is that so bad? I have these urges and they're growing. I need to explore them. Release my inner *Bitch Queen*.'

'What about the other women in the Library, can't they—'

Karen shook her head. 'No, they can't. I know you'd prefer that, and I'm sorry, but part of this is about the power exchange and I do that with the other women in the Library anyway. There's a hierarchy and I'm already at the top. This is bigger than that and for it to be what I need, it has to be with a man.'

Voicing it made plain what she hadn't been able to articulate clearly until that moment. At last Karen understood the growing need burning inside her, sending her to myriad porn sites specialising in Femdom videos.

Silence filled the room.

Karen heard the clock ticking and the rumble of the central heating as it flicked off. She sniffed and caught a whiff of stale beer and crisps from the night before.

'Dan? Say something.'

'I don't know what to say. You've not said this before.'

A little flicker of irritation flared in her belly. 'I have. Not those exact words, but I have. You haven't been listening.' When she saw the hurt in his eyes she pressed on. 'If I never get to play Domme, I'll still be the happiest I've ever been. I'll still live with you and love you and play with the rest of your Library, blessing every day we have together. That won't change. But this is something separate. It's like . . . icing.'

'Icing?'

'On a cake.'

'I know what you mean,' he snapped. 'I just don't like the fact that you compare our relationship to food. Is that all this is to you? Something you can consume and then shit out when you're done?'

She gaped at him. If he sprouted feathers in that moment he couldn't have shocked her more. 'How can you say that? You must know that's not what I meant.'

'If you want more from me just say it. Hell, I've already bought this damn house with you, but if you want more, let me know. Marriage next? Is that it? Are you setting the stage for the next phase in your relationship coup?'

The anger of not long ago flared with in her. She leapt to her feet and snapped the laptop shut, tucking it under her arm. When she next looked at Dan she barely recognised the man standing there. 'You agreed to this. If you don't want to be living here, be a fucking grown up and say it rather than dancing around the bush and blaming me.'

Footsteps pounded the floor to match hers as she marched towards the stairs. Before she could mount them a hand grabbed her wrist.

'Don't run off, Kaz.'

'Fuck you!' She jerked away, twisting as she did so. The slave band twirled around her palm, then snapped. Three broken chains dangled from the rings still circling her fingers.

Dan glared at her.

Karen stared at the bracelet.

Something in her stomach fluttered, then clenched. Horror iced her insides. Then, before it could take hold, fury rolled in again and melted it away.

Laying the laptop down, she snatched off each ring in turn and tossed them at Dan's feet. The bracelet, she unfastened and dropped to join them. 'You'd better take those,' she snarled. 'In case I try to turn them into matching wedding rings.' With the venom of her tone still poisoning the air, she grabbed her laptop, darted up the stairs into the bedroom and slammed the door.

Karen paced the bedroom until its contents became a dizzy blur. Her toes scraped the rug she and Dan had picked together, the pattern of interlocked blue lines around the edge so reminiscent of chains. A pair of Dan's socks lay on the floor, balled up beside the wash basket. Her own dirty underwear draped the edge.

When she threw herself on to the duvet, she caught a whiff of Dan's aftershave, hot and sexy against the cotton. Shrieking, she shoved the duvet on to the floor, wincing when her laptop hit the floor with a dull thud.

Damn it! I'm fucked if that's broken.

She pulled it free and turned it on. The laptop booted with a soft beep to demonstrate its anger, returning to the last page she visited.

Kink4Life.

A small red square with a 'one' inside appeared in her notifications window.

CONVERSATION STARTED WITH BLACK_ANGELUS

She frowned, then opened the private messaging window.

Black_Angelus: Karen? Is that you? I hope it's you.

A tingle raced through her limbs. Just on the edges of her hearing she heard Dan thumping through the bottom of the house. He opened the front door, and she then heard the grind of warped plastic as he wrestled with the external bin. The thunderous clatter of dozens of empty beer and wine bottles broke the air.

She put her fingers to the keys and typed.

Kaz_Kitten: Hi Sith. Yes it's me.

Black_Angelus: Great! Sent six different messages to other 'kittens' B4U. Why R cats so popular?

Kaz_Kitten: Ha, dunno. How are you?

Black_Angelus: Confused. Why did U leave? Something I said? Didn't mean 2 upset U.

Only then did Karen remember the way their conversation ended. Or the way it stopped dead. A twist of shame tightened her lungs and Dan's reaction to it all only made her feel worse.

Kaz_Kitten: No, it was me. Really sorry. Couldn't explain. Not your fault.

Black_Angelus: Explain now?

Kaz_Kitten: Long story.

Black_Angelus: I have time.

Kaz_Kitten: Dan's dad showed up at the Munch.

Black_Angelus: . . .

Black_Angelus: Not that long a story.

Karen laughed aloud.

She heard Dan again, muttering under his breath, something about smelly beer cans and half-eaten cake. The bin opened and closed again.

She kept typing.

Kaz_Kitten: You're right, sorry. Felt longer. But we had to go. Couldn't let him see us.

Black_Angelus: I understand. Dan OK?

She hesitated.

Kaz_Kitten: Freaked, but fine.

Black_Angelus: Good.

The laptop stopped pinging. The natural lull in conversation allowed Karen to consider what she was doing. Something inside her knew this was different to talking to Denise or Henrietta. Chatting with them always led to three way conversations which included Dan, often talking about where they would meet for lunch or the next play party on the Kink4Life calendar.

This had a more covert feel, as though she were talking in the middle of the night, forced to used hushed voices so her parents wouldn't hear.

In that moment, as she heard the front door close, Karen decided she didn't care.

```
Black_Angelus: Good 2 talk 2U 2day. You seem
nice.
```

```
Kaz_Kitten: Thanx.
```

```
Black_Angelus: Talked to others when U left.
Some people interested in playing soon.
```

Karen glared at the screen, stunned at how much the idea angered her. She drummed her fingers against the keys, trying to decide what to say. She was still struggling when Sith sent the next message.

```
Black_Angelus:   Didn't   like   them.   Pushy.
Arrogant. Bet they use dick-pics.
```

A burst of sound came from downstairs. Karen recognised football chanting and realised Dan had decided to watch TV rather than speak to her.

Her fingers prickled. She bit her lip.

Fuck him, then. I'm not fixing it this time. He's the one who needs to apologise.

Karen looked back at the screen to find another line of text.

```
Black_Angelus: Also spoke 2 the guy who arrived
when U left. Dan's dad? Seems nice. Friendly. Is
Dan like him?
```

```
Kaz_Kitten: Usually.
```

```
Black_Angelus: ???
```

```
Kaz_Kitten: Had a fight. Rather not talk about
it.
```

```
    Black_Angelus: Sorry. Won't pry. Still wanna
meet him. Think he will?

    Kaz_Kitten: Don't know.
    Black_Angelus: Ask him. Please? I like U. And
him. Playing would be amazing.
```

She gnawed her thumbnail, listening to the sound of thousands of football fans churning through the sound system downstairs.

```
    Kaz_Kitten: Give me your number.
```

When his response came through, Karen grabbed her mobile and dialled. She heard the line ring and immediately disconnected. As she did, she realised the noise from the TV had lowered and that Dan's footsteps were slowly approaching on the stairs.

```
    Kaz_Kitten: That was me. You have my number
now. I'll call you.

    Black_Angelus: Great. I'd love 2 hear UR voice.

    Kaz_Kitten: I'll call later.

    Black_Angelus: Looking 4ward 2 it.
```

The footsteps approached the room.

```
    Kaz_Kitten: Gotta go. TTFN.
```

She slammed the laptop shut.

Dan opened the door and peered in. 'I'm going to order Chinese. What do you want?'

DAN

Dan dropped his fork on to his plate and glared across the table. Still not looking at him, still tense from her shoulders to her toes, Karen pulled a string of noodles into her mouth with a skilful twist of her chopsticks.

He watched her eat, drinking in the delicate motions of her jaw. The way her lips occasionally pursed to catch a fleck of oil. The way her tongue flicked out to catch juice at the corners.

It was sexy. Every second of it.

He loved watching her eat. He loved watching her do anything, from showering, to parting her hair to add liberal dabs of the minty oil she used to keep it soft.

He thought about apologising but the words wouldn't come.

Instead he snagged a pork rib from the stack liberally slathered with BBQ sauce and attacked one edge with his teeth. As the sauce slid down his chin, her gaze flicked up, touching briefly on the mess before darting away again.

Her lips twisted with distaste.

'What?' he snapped. Dan didn't remember deciding to speak, but now that he had, he couldn't back down. Slamming the gnawed rib onto his plate he wiped his greasy hands down his shirt.

The venomous look Karen shot him in return gave him an absurd rush of pleasure.

Yes, greasy BBQ sauce. Let's see you get that out of my clothes, huh?

Even as he thought it, the absurdity nearly left him reeling.

When did I get so petty?

Karen put down her chopsticks and folded her hands in her lap. 'I didn't say anything. Sir.'

Uh oh.

'Karen?'

'Yes, Sir?'

'You don't have to do that.'

Her eyes flashed. 'No? Because you sure as hell hinted at it earlier, Sir. Seemed to think that I'm your submissive all the time. That I'll do *what*ever you want, *when*ever you want, no matter the issue. That my thoughts and feelings don't matter.'

'I didn't say that.'

'I won't call you a liar, Sir.'

But you'll think it.

He pushed back from the table. 'I'm sorry. Come here.'

Karen immediately slid from her seat and on to the floor. Instead of walking, she crawled, cat-like, on her hands and knees and stopped beside his chair. There she knelt with her head down and her knees spread, hands resting on her thighs, palms turned up.

A true submissive pose.

Dan might have unfastened his trousers immediately if not for the glint in her eye. A submissive pose, yes, but not a submissive woman.

He hesitated. 'Don't do this. Please, let me see your face.'

She looked up, but refused to meet his eyes. Instead she set her gaze on the air beyond his right shoulder. Her lips formed a thin, grim line beneath her furrowed brow.

'Karen—'

'A submissive must never look her Master in the face, nor question is orders. Master's word is law.'

He rolled his eyes. 'Okay, enough. You've made your point.'

Her gaze snapped to his. The sharpness of it made him draw back. 'Have I, *Master*? Because you sure as hell don't seem to. You want everything your way, all the time, but that's not how it works. You certainly don't get to pull the 'Master' card every time you're pissed off. I'm not an actual cotton-picking, sugar-harvesting slave.'

He froze. 'I've never thought that. Who do you think I am?'

She huffed impatiently and drummed her fingertips on the floor. 'I know.' She bit her lip. 'But when we talk about 'slaves' your definition depends on mood.'

This time, Dan was the one to look away. He looked instead at her hand. It seemed naked without the slave band.

The doorbell rang.

Karen bounded to her feet. 'Let me get that, Sir.'

'Kaz, wait.'

But she darted from the kitchen without answering, straight to the front door. He heard it click open. A gasp. A curse. Then the door slammed shut, so hard cutlery rattled against the plates.

When Karen stormed back into the room even the sarcastic show of submission was gone. 'What have you done?'

He gaped. 'What now?'

'Why is Pete here?'

Too late he remembered. His hand fluttered impotently on the table top.

Oh, god.

Her eyes narrowed. 'Why is Pete here *with this*?'

Until that moment he hadn't seen the bag in her hand. She flung it at his face and he ducked, watching the contents sail out to litter the kitchen floor.

A box of condoms. Two lengths of pink, nylon rope. A black leather mask with a zip across the mouth.

What the fuck? Idiot.

He swallowed. 'I can explain that.'

'Can you? Because if you can explain it, it sounds to me like you planned it.'

'You're the one who wanted a male sub.'

'There aren't enough hours in the day to explain all the reasons this is wrong. Don't you dare pin this on me. You can't expect Pete to join us. Especially after last night.' She clapped a hand over her mouth.

'What? What happened last night? With Robert? You said it was fine.'

She growled something under her breath. 'I'm not talking about Robert.'

'Then what? Aside from him saving me from a boot to the head?'

'No, forget that. Back up.' Her voice quivered. 'You thought *Pete* could be my sub?' Another curse, this time as she stared at the trail of sexual paraphernalia across the floor.

'I don't get why you're upset. You're friends already. He's safe. We don't need to vet him first. He's willing to give it a try.'

'*Give it a try*? Dan, this isn't a new flavour of ice cream. Don't you think I should be involved in any plans involving me? When were you planning to let me know?'

'I forgot. We argued—and I was upset, and—'

'When did you arrange it? Was it his idea? I swear, I'll rip him a new—'

Dan rushed forward and caught her arm as she marched to the door. 'It was *my* idea. I thought after last night, and the news about your mum, you could do with a treat.'

'I'm not six years old!' She wrenched her arm away. 'Pete kissed me last night. In the garden. *That's* when Robert found us and *that's* when Pete blurted out that you hit me.'

Dan heard the words but they didn't make sense. They slid through his left ear and poured out his right without processing in between. It felt like a punch to the face. Dan tensed, fumbling for the counter while the world tipped and pitched around him. 'He what?'

Karen seemed to lose some of her fire. She focused on the sink and the pool of grimy water within it. 'That's why Robert was so riled up. He caught Pete trying to force me.'

Still no sense. Pete wouldn't—couldn't—do that.

'He's my best friend,' he said, finally. 'He wouldn't.'

Karen scoffed, glancing into the hallway before returning her gaze to him. 'You don't know your *friend* very well.'

He shook his head. 'I don't get it.'

'He likes me, Dan. Like pining, stalker-style crush. He's been weird since *you* called him to rescue me from that cage without giving me any clothes. I wasn't sure, I doubted myself, but even Sam saw it last night.'

Another shake of the head, as if to do so would stop the words coming. 'No.'

'Yes! Fucking, yes! He kissed me, I tried to get away and he practically tore my clothes.'

'You make him sound like a monster.'

'Not a monster, but he isn't thinking clearly any more. He was pissed off with *you,* Dan. Saying that he's as good as you. That he can control me too if that's what I want.'

Dan wiped the sides of his mouth. 'No. No, this can't be right. A misunderstanding—'

Again she cut across him. 'He spied on us! While we were in here, he watched me give you that hand job. Does that sound like a misunderstanding to you?'

Each word hammered Dan's senses until he felt raw. His body ached, far worse than the bruise on his face, every word almost a physical blow. 'I . . .' He ran his hands through his hair. 'I didn't know. You have to believe me, I had no idea.'

Tears ran down Karen's face. They glistened on her cheeks and fell of the end of her chin to leave tiny damp spots on her top. She stared. 'I didn't want to tell you. I knew it would hurt you, but you're so blind . . . and now this? I had to. You have to know.'

'I'm sorry.'

'That doesn't help me.' She darted out of sight, back into the hallway. Then her footsteps thundered up the stairs.

Dan stared at the goods on the floor, then kicked the box of condoms. He reached the doorway as Karen raced back down, pulling a cardigan over her blouse. 'What are you doing?'

'Going out.'

'Where? It's late.'

'I don't know. Cindy's, maybe. Just away from here.'

'Kaz, please.' He reached for her, but she twisted free like an eel and grabbed her coat from a hook on the wall.

'Don't touch me. I can't think when you touch me. All I want to do is kiss you when you touch me. But I can't right now.' More tears glistened on her cheeks. She wiped them away with the back of her hand, then performed the same motion across her nose.

She looked adorable.

He sucked in a deep breath and grabbed her arm. 'Kaz.' She squirmed in his grip. 'Please listen. I won't touch you or make you do anything, I want to talk to you.'

'No. Let go.' She twisted again.

He tightened his grip.

'Dan, get off me. Please, let me get out of here.' The begging note in her voice did it. Her panic sliced Dan's resolve like a knife. He flexed his fingers. She slid free. Grabbed her keys from another hook. Her mobile.

'Don't call me.' She marched for the door. 'Don't text me. Just leave me alone for a bit.'

Drawn by Karen's movements, Dan looked towards the door for the first time. It hung open, slightly dipped on its hinges. On the other side, Pete loitered on the path, his head lowered.

As she passed him Karen paused long enough to look him up and down.

Pete held out his hand. 'I'm sorry, Karen, I thought—'

She cut him off with a powerful slap to the face. Then, without looking back, Karen stalked onto the street, turned left and vanished from view.

Dan loitered in the hallway, gazing at the wall without seeing. His skin felt hot, too tight for his body. The back of his neck tingled.

'Shit.' He pounded one fist against the wall. Pain lanced through his fingers. He did it again. And again. 'Holy fucking, shit, bollocks!' He hit the wall again and saw a smear of red against the paintwork. He roared wordlessly at the wall.

A gentle hand touched his shoulder.

He spun around. 'You!'

Pete backed off immediately, both hands raised. 'Mate—'

'Don't 'mate' me.'

'I thought you knew. You told me it was okay.'

'Excuse me?'

'On the phone.'

'I was talking about booting Karen's father from the house, not mauling her in our back garden. How could you?'

Pete gripped the back of his neck with both hands. 'I was drunk. I would never normally—probably stoned too.'

The shock and distress faded. It left a deep, yawning void rapidly filled by anger. 'Is it true? Did you spy on us?' He ignored the look of discomfort. 'Did you?'

'I wanted a beer. It was just for a second. I didn't watch the whole time.'

Dan thrust out his hand. He couldn't hear any more. 'What were you thinking?'

Silence. Then Pete narrowed his eyes. 'I was thinking Karen deserves someone good enough to give her everything she needs.'

'How dare you—'

'Oh, bite me,' he snarled. 'Don't get high and mighty because *you* fucked up as much as me.'

'I haven't done anything.'

'Exactly! I look at her and something is missing. This isn't about knowing what she likes, because that stuff isn't important. I can know all her favourite artists, books and music, but she's never going to look at me the way she looks at you. I can accept that. But only if you're looking after her.'

Dan could scarcely breathe. He gazed at his friend through a veil of red and felt his fingers burn with the need to punch something else. Maybe split the knuckles on his other hand. 'You don't know anything about her.'

'I know that when she's smiled lately, it's not how she used to smile. I know that when we all go to the flicks, she's sizing people up in a way I've only ever seen *you* do. Would she do that if she was getting everything she wanted from you? What is it you're not giving her? Is it men? Is that why you invited me tonight? Thought you could get away with another half measure?' He stepped close enough that the hot rush of his breath struck Dan's jaw and neck.

Dan closed his eyes. 'Stop talking, Pete. Right now.'

'Why?' Was it his imagination or did Pete actually sound pleased?

A finger stabbed his chest. He ignored it. Counted to ten. Then again.

'Pete—'

'Don't you like the truth? Can't you handle it?'

'Shut up!' Dan roared. He opened his eyes. Whirled. Struck out. His balled fist struck flesh.

Pete crumpled to the ground, sprawling in the hallway with his legs spread wide. A spot of blood trickled from his left nostril.

Glaring down, Dan longed to punch him again. He wanted to throw his fists around and scream until all the words faded away into white noise he could ignore.

Pete stood and thumbed the blood from his nose. When he next spoke, his voice was rough, clogged with pain. 'Karen deserves more. I've said it before. She loves you, but that love deserves everything you can give her. If you can't do that, then step the fuck away and make space for someone who can. Even if that isn't me.'

He stalked out, abandoning Dan to the thunderous silence.

KAREN

Karen walked three miles before stopping. Tears blurred her vision so completely, she could no longer see. The street lamps above her ranged from dim to off. A car streaked by, music blaring from the open windows, a lively, cheerful beat completely at odds with her own turmoil.

Across the street, a takeaway shop specialising in fried chicken, tossed greasy scents into the air. Her stomach growled and she inwardly cursed herself for leaving her noodles behind.

She patted her pockets. Mobile. Keys. Purse? She groaned. 'Bugger it.' Scrambling for the phone, she flicked through her recent calls and found Cindy's number. Seconds later the line began to ring. And ring. And ring. Eventually Cindy's chirpy voicemail message kicked in, telling her to leave a message that included one deviant sexual secret.

Classic Cindy.

'Hey, I don't know where you are, but I need you. I'm on my way to yours now and I'm on foot. I don't know how long I'll be, but I really hope you're there. Please be there. I can't go home right now. Call me when you get this.'

She hung up and started walking.

After a few minutes Karen began to recognise more of her surroundings. Though relatively new to the area, she knew

Leicester well enough to navigate her way to the flat she once shared with Cindy. Unfortunately that was six miles away.

Karen prepared herself for a long and lonely walk. After half an hour the tears began. She couldn't help it. Thinking of Dan and his stupid, gorgeous face, and the idiot decisions he'd made. It only made her want to turn and run back home. To hug him. To kiss away the gormless look and make him promise to explain his thought process.

Because how could he? What could possibly make him think that Pete was a good idea for a playmate? Even without the disastrous kiss of the night before?

She walked further then became aware her phone was buzzing. When she lifted it from her pocket the number was one she didn't recognise. 'Hello?' she ventured.

'Hi, is that Karen?'

'Speaking. Who is this?' The voice was warm. So familiar.

'It's Sith.'

Karen stopped walking. 'Oh.'

'Sorry, is this a bad time? I meant to call you before, but I didn't know what you were doing. Then I realised that I'd *never* know what you were doing and that now was as good a time as any. I did say I'd call you. Sorry, I'm babbling.'

'Right. Yes, sorry. It's okay, I forgot.'

'Are you okay? I looked forward to hearing your voice but this isn't the voice I remember. You sound like you've been crying.'

She gnawed her bottom lip. 'I have.'

'It *is* a bad time. I'm sorry. Should I go? I'll go.'

'No, wait.' Karen clutched the mobile with both hands. 'Don't go, please. I need to talk to somebody.'

'What is it?'

And the story fell out of her. All of it.

The party. Her mother's terrible news. Her father's appearance. The kiss in the back garden. The punch. She told Sith everything about that day, her conversations with Dan in the car, the munch, then their argument afterwards. The most awkward dinner she had ever experienced and then Pete, showing up at the door wearing that ridiculous leather mask and shouting 'surprise, baby!' as she stepped into view.

By the time the story was over, her throat ached. Weak knees and blurry vision stopped her moving any further and she slumped onto a chipped plastic seat beneath a shattered bus shelter.

'Wow. That was—wow.'

Karen felt a crawling surge of guilt. 'Sorry. I didn't mean to offload like that. We just met.'

'Sounds like you needed it. Where are you?'

She looked left, then right. 'A bus stop on Uppingham Road. I'm trying to get to Highfields.'

Sith sucked in a sharp breath. 'That's miles away. You'll be out there all night.'

'It's fine. I can walk.'

'No.' His voice became firm. 'I can't let you walk all that way. It's not right. Let me pick you up.'

Karen immediately shook her head, even though he couldn't see it. 'Don't let me be a bother.'

'It's no bother. I'll come get you. I live on Lodge Farm Road anyway. I can get to you in five minutes. Where exactly are you?'

'You really don't need to.'

'Do you want me stuck at home wondering if you've been mugged or murdered? Come on, Karen.'

She snickered. 'You'd see justice done, right?'

'I don't know; can you afford me?' A pause. 'Please, Karen. Where are you?'

Sighing, she searched for a road sign. 'Station Road is on my left. On my right is a big park.'

'Manor Field? That's great, don't move. I'll be there in five.' He hung up.

Not knowing what else to do, Karen waited at the stop, kicking her feet back and forth against the dirty pavement.

She watched several packs of teenagers walk by, one cluster most certainly smoking copious amounts of weed, while another talked about nothing but getting their hands on the next dose. Two cars drove by in that time. No busses.

An elderly woman tottered into view and sat beside her, her liver-spotted hands gripping the lead of a small brown ball of fur masquerading as a geriatric terrier. She smiled once and after the second time, took the smile in return as an excuse to start conversation.

'My little Ellie is thirteen years old, y'know.'

Karen sighed inwardly. 'That's sweet. Is she at school?'

The woman gave her a sharp look. 'School? What would a dog be wanting with school?'

Of course she's talking about the damn dog. Heaven forbid it might be a grandchild.

'Finishing school.' She kept her gaze focused forward. 'Some people send their dogs to finishing school to learn things like 'sit,' 'stay,' and 'beg.' Then again, at thirteen she's probably past it now. You know what they say about old dogs and new tricks.'

The woman peered at her through rheumy eyes, clearly trying to decide if she was the butt of some expansive joke.

Karen hoped she wouldn't figure it out.

When a car did finally slow down on the approach, she leapt up and waved frantically. It stopped and Sith stepped out, smiling his dimple heavy smile.

'Hey, Karen. Hop in.'

She did at once, sparing the glaring old lady only a glance as she buckled herself in. As Sith drove on, the woman stood, jerking her dog forward a pace so she could wave her middle finger at the departing car.

Karen caught a glance in the side mirror and stifled a laugh. 'Guess she figured it out.'

The streets sailed by in blurry smudges of orange and black. The deepness of the night eventually gave way to brighter lights as they neared the busier streets of the city centre.

Only then, did Sith speak. 'I'm sorry for what you've been through.'

Karen squirmed in her seat. 'It's fine.'

'But your mother . . .'

'She's a fighter; if she's going to go, she'll do it kicking and screaming. And we'll have good times before she goes.'

'If you need anything,' he murmured. 'Advice. Questions answered.'

She looked a question at him.

'My aunt, three years ago. Cervical cancer. By the time they found it there was nothing anyone could do.'

'I'm sorry.'

He shrugged. 'I'm okay. I won't lie, you never fully recover, but I'm okay.'

Karen watched his profile. She waited for him to turn but he never did, his gaze focused straight ahead, never wavering, never flickering. Eventually he took the road alongside the retail park and eased on to St George's Way, passed the Phoenix Cinema. From the corner of her eye she saw the time flashing at the top of the Mercury Building, the large red numbers glittering in the night. Then the display changed to show the temperature. Two degrees.

She silently thanked Sith for his insistence in coming to get her. Her coat and thin blouse beneath were simply not thick enough to withstand that sort of cold, even with the cardigan in between.

As he eased onto London Road, she gave him directions, steering him into the deepest depths of Highfields.

Ten minutes later Sith stopped outside a thickset flat of dirty grey stone with dingy lights gleaming in a sporadic pattern across the windows. He sighed. 'Here? You're sure?'

'Cindy and I used to live here. Now she shares with her girlfriend.'

'But she didn't answer when you called?'

'No.' Karen grinned. Tried to. 'Probably busy spiking Sam's food.' She caught Sith's curious look. 'Sorry, private joke.' She patted his knee and offered a small smile. 'Thanks, Sith. You're really sweet.'

'My pleasure.' He seemed to want to say more, but when he didn't, Karen clambered out the car and flicked the door shut. As she hurried up the steps he called to her. 'I'll wait until you go in.'

The urge to tell him not to bother rose strong within her, but he was unlikely to listen anyway. Nodding, she pressed the buzzer for number three.

Silence.

Karen stared at the grimy front door and the spiderweb of cracks through the glass. Inside, the hallway was dark but for a flickering light off to the right hand side. The acrid scent of stale urine and weed flooded her nostrils until she ducked the lower half of her face into the upturned collar of her coat.

She rang again. 'Come on, Cindy. Please.'

Another ring. This time she kept her finger on the buzzer, listening to the sharp sound echo through the intercom beneath the panel of buttons.

'Everything okay?' Sith's voice chased her up the steps.

'It's fine. I'll ring her. She's probably asleep.' But as she went through the motions Karen knew Cindy wasn't in the flat. Even the lights in the windows were off. She stepped back long enough to check. They were easy to recognise, having leaned out of them many a night to escape the fumes of Cindy's chain smoking habit.

Again the phone switched to voicemail.

'Damn it, Cindy, I need you. Please open the door.'

A gentle hand touched her shoulder. She spun around, but it was only Sith, gazing at her with a kind, sad smile. 'She's not here, Karen.'

Tears stung her eyes. Frustration, she told herself. Not self-pity and certainly not distress at her sudden loneliness. 'I've nowhere else to go. I can't go home—I don't want to see Dan right now.'

'Don't you have any other friends?'

The question cut deeper than Karen ever realised it could. 'Of course I do. But not that I can stay with. There are people from university. People in the same research building as me.'

'Those aren't friends, Karen. What about those two from the munch? They seemed nice.'

'They aren't local. They'll be heading home by now.'

Sith massaged her shoulders. 'Come on.'

'Why? Where, Sith? Where the hell am I going?' It wasn't fair to snap at him, she knew that. But the frustrations of the day were catching up to her.

'Come with me.' He smiled again. The dimples pricked his cheeks and gave him the air of a cheeky five-year-old. 'I'm not leaving you out here by yourself.'

'I'll sit in a pub. Maybe grab a drink. Or six.'

'If you could afford a drink you would have called a cab here rather than walking. Let me help you.'

She looked up into his bright hazel eyes and saw genuine concern there. The need to help. The *desire* to help.

'I can't.'

'Why? If you want a drink, I have lots. I'm a rum drinker but I'm sure I can rustle up something else if you prefer. You'll be indoors. Warm. Then, when you're ready, I'll drop you off wherever you like.'

The tears stopped threatening and proceeded to slide down her cheeks. 'You're so nice. Why are you being so nice?'

'I like you.' His hand left her shoulder and drifted up, the pads of his fingers brushing her cheek. He wiped away the tears. 'Let me help.'

'What about Dan?'

His gaze darkened. 'I'm not offering to take you home so I can ravish you. I just want to get you somewhere warm so you can relax after a hard day. I like you, but I'm not a monster.'

Mortified, she leapt to correct him. 'I didn't mean that.'

'You're nervous, fine. You met me this morning and already you've sat in my car and let me drive you around. But I'm not a madman, a rapist or a murderer. I'm not even a Tory; I only vote Green.' The smile touched his lips again. 'I'm a barrister.'

'In training,' she added with a sniff.

'I'm not going to do, or expect anything of you. Let me take you home.'

Again she searched his face, for some sign of deceit or untruth. Nothing.

Karen sighed. 'Fine. Let's go.'

DAN

Dan looked up from the wreckage of his dinner and tried to figure out what he'd heard.

Doorbell? At this hour? Who the hell is that?

He glanced at his mobile and saw the time was far later than he thought. Karen had been gone for hours.

But she wouldn't knock.

He got up, stepping gingerly through the shards of broken plates to reach the hallway. A shadow fell on the carpet through the double glazed glass.

'Who is it?' he called.

'Robert Owusu.'

Dan scrubbed his eyes. Then his ears. 'Who?'

'Robert. I want to see mi girl.'

If the rough, Caribbean accent wasn't enough, the demand for Karen filled in the blanks. Karen's father stood at the door, though what he hoped to achieve Dan couldn't hope to guess.

He strode up to the door and flung it open. 'She's not here. Go away.'

Rather like the night before, Robert Owusu loomed in the door frame like an over-sized wrestler. Instead of his wide-brimmed hat he wore a leather flat cap with stripes of black, yellow and green around the rim. His gold teeth glinted in the half light.

'Go away? That so, Silver Fox? Not til I speak to mi daughter.'

'I told you, she's not here. And even if she was, I don't think she'd want to speak to you.'

'I don't often take no for an answer. Wasn't last night lesson enough?'

Dan gritted his teeth. 'Last night showed me nothing more than exactly why Karen lied about you. She told me you were dead, did you know that?'

The golden glint vanished. 'She wouldn't.'

'Oh, really? Now for the last time, she's not here. If you want her, ring her mobile, but leave me the hell alone.'

Robert's gaze flicked over him, stopping briefly on the yellowing bruise on the side of his face. Though he longed to look away Dan refused, holding firm and even tilting his face to show off the mark. 'Yes, it's a good one. Well done, you. Bravo. Attacking someone in their house with no provocation. I should have you arrested.'

'I was protecting mi girl. You hit her.'

'Did you hear her say that? Has she said anything of the kind to you? I've never hit her, Mr Owusu, nor will I ever. I'm not a violent man.' As he spoke he shifted his bloodied hand behind the partially open door.

'Mr Owusu,' Robert chuckled. He flipped off his hat and rubbed a hand through those impossibly black dreadlocks. 'No one has called mi that for years. You make mi feel young.'

'Good for you. Now are you leaving, or do I need to call the police?'

'No, I'm going. When Karen comes, you tell her to call mi. Mi want to speak about her mother.'

'Charlaine?' Dan felt a sudden stab of guilt. 'What happened?'

'Nothing. She wants mi to make peace with the girl. Hopes I'll do it before she passes.'

'That's important to her?'

'It's important to *me*.' Robert slapped his chest with a meaty hand. 'I know I did wrong by Charlaine, but she took mi back anyway. Least I can do now is make good with our little girl. It's only right she sees us kiss and hug before she don't see nothing no more. I want to do that for her.'

For long seconds Dan stared at the bigger man wondering what to say. Then he stepped back and held the door open. 'Come inside.'

Two minutes later they sat in the kitchen, Dan nursing a mug of tea, Robert staring at the crushed crockery with mild interest.

'You two have a fight?'

'Yes. No. Yes, we did, but that's not what this is. I did this myself.'

'And yuh hand?'

Dan glanced at his battered knuckles. 'I punched the wall.'

'Ah, so that's the blood smear. Gym, Silver Fox. Or a punching bag. Kinder to the knuckles.'

'Please stop calling me that. My name is Daniel.'

A shrug. Then, 'What did yuh fight about?'

'None of your business.'

'Was it me?'

He slammed his mug against the table. 'I invited you here to wait for Karen. I don't want to talk about my private life.'

'She usually fights with her boyfriends about mi. They decide they should meet mi and she says no. Guess she solved that problem by saying I'm dead. Cruel, cruel child.'

'I can see why she did it. You're an arse.'

Robert raised his eyebrows. 'Silver Fox shows some life after all. Why you say that?'

The memory of it made him cringe. Bite his lip. 'You cheated on your wife.'

'Charlaine tell you that?'

'Karen.'

'Ah. Mi baby girl be smart, but she don't always see what's right under her nose. I never cheated on nobody. Charlaine and I—we wasn't together when I saw those other women. How can I cheat on somebody who has no claim on me?'

'You're married.'

'Divorced,' he corrected. 'Years ago. And like an addict I came back for more. No matter how many women I saw, none were so damn fine as Charlaine. I didn't want nobody else.'

'Did you ever tell her that?'

Robert glanced up. Cocked an eyebrow. 'Tell her what?'

'That you missed her. Wanted her.'

'No. She was mi woman. *Is* mi woman. I don't need to tell her that. She knows.'

'Right. And if she did the same as you, would you take her back?'

'Ha, you're a funny man.' He swept off his hat, rubbed his head, then replaced it, all in one smooth move. When he looked up again his gaze hardened. 'My women know better than to act like that.'

'Your women . . . they're not cattle, you do realise?'

'Think you're funny, do you? No, they're not cattle, but they're mine. Charlaine? Mine. Karen? Mine. I won't stand such foolishness from them. They're better than me.'

Dan stared at the older man as though seeing him for the first time. In a curious, backhanded way, he saw his own thoughts and feelings reflected in Robert Owusu. Out dated thoughts on the place of women.

He felt sick.

'I don't know Charlaine very well, but Karen certainly is better than you. Better than me. Us being men doesn't give us special powers or rights, Mr Owusu. What you did was wrong.'

'We was divorced.' Robert insisted. 'And I love that woman. I don't show it well but I do. I want Karen to understand that.'

Dan rolled his eyes. 'Can't help you there.'

'You can. She listens to you.'

'Not recently.'

Silence.

Then, 'I don't miss much. I'm old and randy but I see a lot. Your hand, the wall, your floor. I also see you, Silver Fox. Daniel.'

At the use of his name Dan couldn't help but look up. He caught the older man staring at him, expression weary, but solemn.

'You love my girl. What she sees in you, I'll never know, but she loves you too. If I want to make peace with her I need to be a part of her life. So I need to be part of yours.' He pulled a tatty lottery ticket from his pocket and a stubby blue pen, the kind stuck in the small holes drilled into tables bolted down at the local bookies. He scribbled a line of numbers then shoved the ticket over.

'When she comes back, call mi. She won't do it, so don't bother asking. Just tell her I came and call mi. Will you do that?'

He hesitated, then gathered up the ticket and tucked it into his pocket. 'Sure.'

'Thank you. That's all mi want.' Robert got up and walked to the door. Before passing through he said; 'Put that hand in some ice or you won't be able to move your fingers tomorrow.'

Seconds later the front door opened then closed again.

Dan groaned, running his hands over his face and through his hair. The fine strands caught in the flesh of his mangled knuckles and he bit back a wince.

No ice, but the handy bag of peas that did so well on his face the night before, felt good against his hand. Cold quickly numbed the agony.

With the other hand he flipped out his phone. Dialled. The call went straight to voice mail. 'Karen, I know you said don't call, but I need to speak to you. Please come home.' He hung up.

Simple. Straight forward. To the point. No begging, no pleading, no drunken babbling. Not like last time.

Last time, ha!

Last time he drank himself silly, throwing up in the kitchen sink after, an argument with Karen. Neither of them were impressed by that. Last time he let her go and nearly lost everything at Sugar Dust when his ex, Beth showed up, dragging up stories from the past. Last time he begged. He pleaded. He did everything except actually act in a way that gave Karen a reason to stay.

Dan sat straighter in his chair.

Even Robert put aside other women to go back to Charlaine. It's what she *wanted. And he gave it to her.*

The first aid kit proved easy to find. Yet another legacy of Karen's organisational skills. Wrapping the hand was no mean feat, but he did it and knotted the end using a combination of his left hand and his teeth. When sure it was secure, he snatched up his keys and darted from the house.

It took twenty minutes to reach the flats where Karen once lived. As he pulled up to the gloomy block of grey concrete, his gaze swivelled upwards, searching for the dim blue light in the window as he had so many times before. No blue light. No yellow light. No light at all in fact, and when he leaned on the buzzer he had no choice but to admit the truth. She wasn't there. Nobody was.

Out came the mobile again. He straightened when Cindy answered. 'I Karen with you?'

'What?' Thunderous music poured through the ear piece. Several shrill voices raised in unison, sung along to some pop track from twelve years ago. 'Dan?'

'Is Karen with you?'

'One sec, I'll go outsi—no you silly bitch, get off me. I'm with her. No, *her*. Her too if you like, but I'm not interested.' The music faded slightly. 'Jesus, there are some desperate folk out tonight. Wait a minute, Dan.'

He had no choice but to do exactly that, wandering back to the car since nobody was in the flat. Back in his seat, he tapped the fingers of his uninjured hand against the wheel and waited.

The music died completely.

Cindy's voice roared into his ear. 'There, I'm—oops. Sorry. My ears are ringing. Am I shouting?'

Dan placed the phone on the dashboard and brushed the screen to switch it to speaker. 'No, go ahead.'

'You said something about Karen?'

'She's not with you?'

'At Helsinki? No, I thought she was with you.'

'She left.'

A pause. When Cindy spoke again, her voice growled low and feral. 'What the hell have you done now?'

'Long story.'

'You must be the absolute master of relationship cock-ups. No pun intended of course.'

He huffed a breath that might be interpreted as laughter. 'Thanks.'

'How long ago did she leave?'

'I don't know. Two hours ago? Three? I've lost track. I hoped she was with you.'

'I've been out all day. Damn it, I knew I should have made her keep her key. Where else would she go? What about Daphne's place?'

Dan stared out the window until the trees and parked cars merged into a grey blur. He pumped his foot against the brake pedal to think. Eventually he shook his head. 'Don't worry, Cindy, I've got this.'

'I wouldn't worry, but *you* called *me*, dick-face. Now I'll do nothing *but* worry about it.'

'It's fine, honestly—'

'Shut up. In fact, get off the line so I can call her.'

He hung up, lowering his head to bump his forehead on the steering wheel.

Where would she go?

There were a few places: a late night independent bookstore that doubled as a coffee shop, several pubs. Though as he thought about it more, Dan felt sure she wouldn't go to those places alone.

The bookstore perhaps, but not a pub.

He restarted the car and began driving, aiming for the ring road that would lead him into town. On the way, he jammed his bluetooth receiver into his ear and began to call his other subs. Though slim, there was a chance Karen had turned to them. Since Cindy was the obvious choice, it made sense to avoid her flat if Karen didn't want to be found.

After speaking briefly with both Hannah and Rebecca, each claiming they'd seen nothing of Karen since their last play session, Dan stopped the car outside an old, converted church and tried to think.

The phone rang in his hands. 'Cindy?'

'She left two voice mails begging me to let her in. She was in tears, Dan. What have you done? And don't you dare say it's a long story. I'll rip your tiny cock off, I swear to God.'

He sighed. 'You have such a way with words.'

'Tell me!'

He did.

KAREN

Karen cradled her tumbler to her chest and watched Sith walk across his living room. It was large, compact and neat, like him, though signs of his true personality occasionally peeped through, Pictures on the sideboard lots of smiling faces, probably family; a stack of sports magazines half sliding off a coffee table; a large wicker basket beneath the radiator with a purple blanket bunched up inside.

The owner of the blanket, a tiny, honey-yellow cat, purred and slithered in and around his ankles. When he tripped over her for the third time, Sith scooped her up and put her gently outside. The look she gave him as the door closed was nothing short of guileless disbelief.

'She's always like that when I have guests.'

'Possessive?'

'Protective. She thinks everyone is out to get me.'

Karen grinned. 'Makes me wonder what sort of people you usually bring here.'

Sith hesitated. 'Friends. You know, law people. A girl every now and then. A man.'

Tracing a pattern on the edge of the sofa, Karen murmured, 'Do they stay?'

'Sometimes.' Sith stopped near the coffee table, his abrupt motion causing the magazines to slide to the floor. He cursed and snatched them up, forming an untidy wedge, that he shoved onto the bottom shelf of a tall bookcase against the far wall. 'Sorry it's such a mess.'

She arched an eyebrow. '*This* is a mess?'

'For me it is.' After shuffling a trio of remote controls into a line beside the TV, he finally sat on the floor near her feet. He snagged his own glass off the table and raised it. 'Cheers.'

'Cheers.' The rum brought a pleasant warmth to her chest and burned on the way down. It reminded her of hot summer days and late dinners in the conservatory, while her mother played soft classical music.

Sith touched her knee. 'Are you comfortable?'

Karen giggled. She wriggled her toes within the confines of her socks, stretching once then relaxing as she tucked her legs beneath her. The fluffy blanket draped over her chest flopped down to cover her knees. 'All you need to do is tuck me in, give me a good book and I'll never leave. You don't have to do this.'

'I know.' He gazed at her, one hand toying with a sea shell threaded through one of his dreadlocks. 'I want you to be comfortable in my house, that's all.'

'Is that why you're on the floor?'

'I'm more comfortable here.'

Karen ran a finger around the rim of her glass. 'When I'm home with Dan, just relaxed and casual like we are now, he sometimes makes me sit on the floor. He gets me a blanket and a cushion, or whatever else I might want, but he puts me at his feet. Just another way of maintaining the D/s.'

Sith looked away. Cleared his throat. Fussed with his dreadlocks some more, then took a swift glug of rum. 'Do you like doing that?'

'Not all the time. Most of the time I just want to sit on the damn sofa and away from the laminate floor. But he's good at gauging that. He never asks me to if he senses I'm not in the mood. He's good like that.'

'What happens afterwards? Do you play?'

'Generally, no. We get on with whatever else we need to do with our day. He'll read a case study. I'll make some research notes. It sometimes leads to a blow job, but not normally.'

'You said you're his slave?'

'Sub, slave; we use the words interchangeably.'

Something dark passed across Sith's eyes. 'I want to ask but I don't want you to think that I'm . . . '

Karen waited. Though she could hazard a guess, she wanted to hear him say it. She wanted to hear how he handled such a delicate subject.

'Is race involved?' he said, at last. 'Some people on *Kink4Life* enjoy playing up the racial aspect of a mixed relationship. Do you play up to the historical background?'

Delicately put. Spoken like a true lawyer.

She quirked an eyebrow. 'You mean does he like to pretend that he's worked me in the cotton fields all day before bringing me home to rape?'

Sith frowned. 'You don't have to be so—'

She cut him off with a raised hand. 'Sorry, you're right. That was shitty of me. But I get asked that a lot and only by black men. They seem to want to save me.'

'You don't want to be saved?'

'I don't *need* to be saved.' She put the glass down beside the sofa. 'We never play that game. We might roleplay cat and owner, teacher and student, doctor and patient, but never that. He finds it as distasteful as I do.'

'But the word slave—'

'—is just a word. It has extremely negative overtones when Dan uses it in unsuspecting company, but most people understand that's not what our relationship is about. Though he does look sexy cracking a whip.'

A wide grin spread Sith's lips. For the first time, she noticed the gap between his front teeth, small, but there. It made him look even cuter. If that were possible.

'I'd like to see that one day. Not to be involved—I know he doesn't like that—but does he ever let people watch? Like at play events?'

'Occasionally. More so recently. He enjoys showing off his control. Lucky for him, I do too. I think that's part of his problem with the idea of me being Domme over someone else. He can't control that.'

Leaning back, Sith crossed his arms over his stomach and stretched out his legs. 'Of course he can. You just need to be creative.' He beckoned. 'I'll show you.'

The words set off an instant spark in Karen. His closeness, his soft voice, the gentle, relaxed drift of her mind brought on by the two glasses of rum she enjoyed before this one.

She licked her lips, twitching her legs free of the blanket and swinging them to the ground. Blanket next, untucked from her body and draped neatly over the arm of the sofa.

Stop stalling. This doesn't mean anything, just go. Talk to him.

Sith faced away from her, but his right hand was up in the air, palm flat, waiting to take her fingers into his. Though his shoulders and neck appeared loose and relaxed, something about his energy suggested the exact opposite.

She watched the back of his neck for some sign of his intent but he didn't turn. Just waited. As if he knew she would come. The realisation made her stomach clench, made the secret juncture between her legs grow warm and moist. That expectation of obedience was familiar and an unexpected comfort after such a stressful night.

Karen put her hand in his and let Sith tug her to the ground. After a bit of fumbling he sat her in his lap, facing him, with her legs bent up on either side of his body.

Even clothed, Karen felt exposed. Her nipples stiffened against her bra and begged for attention. She swallowed and focused on his chin.

'Imagine I'm your master,' he said.

The words brought her gaze up, hard and fast. Her breathing quickened and when Sith gazed into her eyes, the rest of the room faded away. She saw nothing but his face. Heard nothing but his voice.

'Master?' she croaked.

'Yes. Can you imagine that?'

Jesus . . . I think I can . . .

Her tongue felt thick and clumsy, so she settled for nodding.

Sith smiled. 'Good. Imagine that. And imagine that we're naked.'

Oh, boy . . .

'We're not actually naked, Karen. I'm just trying to explain. Is that okay?' He didn't move or touch her, his hands now flat on the floor to either side of his hips.

Karen wished he would put them on her waist. 'Okay. Go on.'

'Imagine we're naked and you're sitting here, waiting for me to enter you.'

The calm way he spoke sent muddled messages to Karen's brain. She swayed and convulsively gripped his shoulders against falling. When he smiled, her skin began to tingle. He grasped her forearms to hold her hands in place.

'I enter you. I put your arms here so you can hold on and I give you control over depth and speed. But you know at any moment I can tell you to move faster or slower. And you'll obey. You'll have to.'

Karen pushed her hips forward. A small motion, but it spread her legs further and pressed the crotch of her jeans deeper between her legs. The pressure made her whimper. Comfort and familiarity lurked just out of reach. Sith's words and soothing voice promised solace in the form of control. *His* control. He would take responsibility for everything and leave her free to enjoy the moment. Free to relax. Free to feel. No need to assess, consider, analyse or decide. No need to ponder alternatives, or plan for the actions of others. Absolute freedom of responsibility. That's what a master offered. That's what his voice promised.

It would be so easy to let him take over. To follow orders as she often did and let someone else take charge of making everything better.

'I'd have to.' She tightened her grip.

'You have to,' he corrected. Sith's hands touched her shoulders, then skimmed along the length of her arms. He teased his fingers into the crook of each elbow then held her wrists between his thumbs and forefingers. When he lifted, Karen moved with him, allowing him to lift her arms out from her body and up to shoulder height.

When he let go, she held her position.

He grinned. 'Good girl.'

The words sent an electric thrill through her body. They always did.

She closed her eyes and listened for his body motions, his breathing, his sighs.

A warm gust of rum-scented air whispered over her cheek and then his lips touched her closed eyelids one by one. Her nose. Her cheeks. Her mouth. A chaste touch, barely a brush of his lips against hers, but it lit a fire in Karen's body that burned hotter and brighter with every passing second.

She jumped as cool fingers traced the neckline of her blouse. One finger trailed down, dipping briefly into the valley of her bra, before returning and fiddling with her buttons. One popped open. Then another. Another.

Soon her blouse lay open and Karen shivered in the sudden rush of cool air against her chest and stomach.

A groan from Sith pulled her eyes open. 'You're stunning,' he murmured.

Saying 'thank you' didn't seem right. Saying nothing felt rude. Karen settled on a compromise. 'Then what?'

Sith's smile brightened. He lowered his head and nuzzled his face against her breasts, flicking out his tongue to lick the tops of each one. When she moaned, he dipped one hand into the left cup and pinched the solid nub of her erect nipple.

She gasped and bucked her hips against him, straining for more. *Needing* more.

This was so much easier. Losing herself in the strength of his control. No need to think. No need to analyse.

'Go on.' She begged shamelessly, giving herself over to him with the single desperate plea.

He wasn't slow to accept.

His hands returned to her shoulders, pressing down. Pliant and obedient she slid down his legs until her face reached his waistband. Slowly, he unfastened his belt.

Karen watched the hypnotic display with half-lidded eyes. When he tucked the buckle into his fist and wound the strap around his hand, she had a brief moment to wonder what came next, before the flat end of the belt slapped against her arse. The stinging impact made her gasp and lower her head, instinctively flicking out her tongue to lick the hot shaft that normally rose to meet her.

It wasn't there. Just the unfastened buttons of Sith's jeans and his gentle hands against her head.

He was clearly erect. Bulging, straining for release from the tightness of those jeans. A single button remained. One tiny nub of metal hiding his underwear from view.

He pushed down on her head. 'Go on. You know what to do.'

The words were so familiar. The voice soft and commanding. So much like Dan's and yet not.

Not. He's not Dan.

The moment the thought materialised, Karen rushed back into herself. The giddy rush of losing herself leaked away and she stared at Sith, watching his chest rise and fall.

He licked his lips. 'What are you waiting for?'

She jerked upright. 'No.'

He froze.

'You're not Dan. You're not my master. I can't do this with you.'

Sith immediately dropped the belt. He scrabbled into a stable sitting position and fastened the top buttons of his jeans. 'But I thought—didn't you want—'

'I did.' She raised a hand to stop him digging a verbal pit neither of them would be able to escape. 'But I can't. I'm sorry.'

'You wanted to submit. You said it. I thought that's what you wanted.'

'It is. I do.'

He ruffled his hand through his hair and shrugged. 'Then what?'

'I want to submit *to Dan,*' she said. 'It's not about *submission*, it's about *him*. It's always been about him. I'm not a natural submissive, Sith. I don't know how, but you *knew* that as soon as we met. I tried to deny it but that's stupid. All my other relationships failed because I like to lead. But not with him; never with Dan.'

Sith fumbled with his jeans once more, then covered himself with his hands. 'I don't understand.'

'Dan tops me in a way no one else ever could. I don't know why, but he's perfect. And I need that, Sith. But no on else can do it. With anyone else I want the power. It's there. It's in me. It's an instinct.'

'What does that mean?'

It means I should leave. It means I should get up and leave this house before I do something really stupid.

Instead she said, 'Stand up.'

He did. Slowly. Watching her face, tense all over, as though ready to bolt at any moment.

'Put your arms behind your head.'

He hesitated.

'Do it.' She hadn't meant to snap. The order burst from her mouth with a whip-crack snap and Sith leapt to attention, as though poked with a live cattle prod. He threaded his fingers and held the back of his head. He stared at her, mouth agape, chest heaving. And it was perfect. So perfect.

Karen's distant yearning for something more roared forwards like a tidal surge. Her body hummed with it and the moist juncture between her legs throbbed and urged her on.

She closed the small space between them. Touched his chest.

His pectorals were solid beneath her fingers, defined in a way that suggested weights training and an impeccable diet. She traced her hands down his ribs and found the flat plane of his stomach. Each abdominal showed the same definition as his chest.

With both hands she grabbed the bottom of his t-shirt and dragged it up over his head. The sleeves caught on his elbows and the neck gathered under his chin but she didn't drag it all the way. Instead she left the fabric over his face, blocking his vision and leaving his torso utterly exposed. His arms shuddered but didn't move.

'Very good,' she murmured.

He sighed, the gust of his breath causing a billow in the t-shirt fabric.

Karen kissed his chest, lathing her tongue around one tiny nipple while pinching the other. When he groaned, she switched and nibbled at the other sensitive bud of skin. His knees buckled.

'This feels more natural,' she whispered. 'I could do this all day.' Scraping her nails first up then down his stomach, she watched him twitch and shudder. When she unfastened his jeans and shoved them down to his knees, she saw the long line of his cock pressed against the front of his Calvin Klines.

'Karen—'

'No.' She cut him off with another teasing scratch of her nails down his chest. 'Be quiet.'

She dropped to her knees, steadying herself with her hands on his hips. Unlike Dan's, Sith's belly was hard and smooth, with not the smallest wisp of hair.

She looked lower, watching a small damp patch form on his boxers. Beneath it his cock twitched and grew, straining to reach her face. Breathing against him dragged a strangled gasp from his throat.

'Oh, God,' he murmured. 'Yes, please.'

Karen knew that voice. She knew the song of desperation sung by a submissive on the very brink of what they wanted most. She knew because she sang it with Dan while he teased her with the promise of an orgasm. Dangling release before her but never quite within her grasp.

The musky aroma of Sith's arousal filled Karen's nose and fired every synapse in her body dedicated to sexual pleasures. When he jerked towards her, his skin brushed her nose and dragged a low whimper from them both.

What am I doing? I can't—what sort of person am I?

It was wrong. All of it.

She stood. Yanked the t-shirt back over Sith's head. Allowed it to drop into place.

Beneath it his eyes were closed. They popped open as the fabric left his face and he stared at her with eyes slightly glazed in the dim light.

'I'm sorry,' she murmured. 'I don't know how many times I'm going to say that tonight, but I really am. I can't do this either.'

'Karen.' He looked ready to beg. 'Please.'

'I can't, Sith. This is better, but there's still something missing.'

The lust in his eyes dimmed. Like shutters slamming closed, his expression darkened and left something cold and angry. 'What exactly do you want from me?'

'I don't want anything from you. It's from Dan.'

DAN

Dan parked the car and leaned his head against the steering wheel. His mind still buzzed, reeling with the force of Cindy's rage. He fought the urge to check over his shoulder, telling himself that she couldn't possibly have made it here after so short a time. But it would be like her.

Threats were all well and good, but Cindy wouldn't be Cindy without following through. He wondered if he would ever be safe again.

If Karen shows up perhaps.

A glance at the house dropped his spirits even lower. No lights in the windows. No sign of movement. No . . . there was something. Someone sitting on the step by the front door.

Scrambling from the car, Dan slammed the door and ran up the path. 'Karen?'

'No, mate. Sorry.'

He stopped. Glared. 'What are you doing here?'

Pete stood and rubbed a hand through his hair. 'I want to talk to you.'

'I've nothing to say to you.'

'Come on, Dan.'

'No. It's Karen I need to talk to, not you.'

'So our friendship doesn't mean anything?'

Dan felt the tiniest twinge of guilt. 'That's not what I said.'

'It feels like it. I've cocked up. I know that, but I'm here to fix it and I can only do that if you let me.'

'What can you possibly say?'

Pete rubbed his arms. 'Can we go inside? It's freezing and I've been sitting out here for half an hour.'

A pause. Then a grunt. 'Whatever.' Dan pushed passed him and unlocked the door, stamping into the hallway. He flicked on lights as he walked, finally entering the living room and flopping into an armchair.

Pete followed a few paces after, loitering in the doorway. 'Can I sit?'

'Sure. Why not.'

He perched on the arm of the sofa and fiddled with his fingers.

In the light, faint discolouration showed around his jaw. Almost a mirror for Dan's but nowhere near as broad and angry as Robert's handy work. The guilt worming through Dan's insides became an insistent burrowing.

'Do you want some peas, or something? For your face?'

Pete touched his jaw, winced, then shrugged. 'I'm fine.'

'You'll bruise.'

'It'll make me look butch. I don't mind. But then, it probably won't; you hit like a girl.'

'Tell Karen that.'

Pete smirked. 'She'd give me a matching bruise on the other side.'

Silence. Then, 'What do you want, Pete?'

'To fix this. We've been friends for years. Something like this can't just stomp on all that time. I thought we were stronger than that.'

'I thought so too.'

'What I did—I'll never forgive myself for that. It was the stupidest thing I've ever done. Karen isn't—she deserves better than some creep mauling her while drunk. I still can't believe it. I don't know how far it would have gone either, if Robert hadn't turned up. I might have done something really awful.'

'As opposed to *kinda* awful?'

'I'm trying to apologise, here.'

'You're doing a shitty job.'

'I'm sorry! I know it's no excuse, but I really feel for her. I think I love her.'

Dan surged to his feet. 'Get out.'

'No, wait—'

'Out. Get the fuck out.' Dan dashed forward, grabbing Pete by the scruff of his jacket. The other man struggled, but Dan put everything he had into pushing, driving him towards the front door.

Just before the step Pete dug in his heels and leaned back. Dan stumbled. It felt like shoving a brick wall.

'Jesus, what do you weigh?'

'I don't know. Twelve stone?'

'More like forty.'

'Screw you; I'm just not a weak-arse fairy like you. I haul sheets of glass and metal siding for a living. Get off me.'

'Get out of my house.'

Pete sighed and leaned back again, a quick nudge but it sent Dan sprawling. He crashed into the wall and bumped twice before able to stop himself. Growling, he launched forward again, a rugby tackle around Pete's middle that took them both outside. They landed hard, rolling off the path and on to the gravel beneath the window. As he flailed, Dan's legs tangled in the ivy crawling up the arching trellis and dragged it down.

Beneath him, Pete scrambled and squirmed. 'I'm not leaving until I've said my piece.'

'I don't want to hear anything you have to say.' A hand clamped over his face and pushed, twisting until he had no choice but to release his grip on Pete's waist. The other man followed him over, flipping them until Dan lay crushed beneath, gravel crunching under his head.

'You should. No one else is going to call you out on your shit and it's going to leave both of you unhappy. Especially Karen.'

'Stop talking about Karen,' Dan roared, lashing out with his fist. His knuckles caught a glancing blow on Pete's jaw before thudding off his collar bone. Heaving up with one knee, he rolled them again, landing on top. He pressed down with both hands on the other man's shoulders. 'After what you did you have no right.'

'And *you* do? I came to say sorry, but you still won't admit you're being a shitty Dom, let alone a shitty boyfriend.'

'I'm a great Dom!'

Another heave from Pete. Dan yelped as he went sailing over Pete's head, crashing into the big bin on the far side of the gravel. Thankfully full, it rocked on its wheels a few times before stabilising. When he stood, it rocked a few more times, forcing him to steady it. Then he rushed at Pete again.

It was a clumsy attack. Fighting had never been a strong point of Dan's, but this seemed like a good point to try. With rage filling every limb, burning through his very marrow, he wanted nothing more than to expend it on something. Anything. Anyone.

This time Pete didn't take the tackle but lurched to the side. Dan stumbled forward and hit the remnants of the trellis, tangling his legs in it and tumbling over.

'Doms are supposed to look after their subs.'

'What the hell do you know about it?'

'Enough to know you're not doing your job. Giving her what she needs so long as it tallies with what *you* want isn't enough. What about what *she* wants?'

Dan thrust out his legs, hooking Pete around the knees. When the other man fell, he scrambled up and sat on his stomach, knees pinning his arms to the floor. 'I always give her what she wants.'

'Including me?'

Dan froze, hand pulled back for another punch. 'What?'

'You always give her what she wants, was that me too? Did she ask you for me?'

'You're missing the point. She asked for a sub, so I gave her a sub.'

Pete jerked up with his hips and heaved his arms off the gravel. Wobbling, Dan had no balance left to counter when his friend pushed him back again. He hit the gravel hard and lay there panting.

'I'm not a sub, Dan. I'm just a guy who got curious about what his friend was up to. I don't like pain and it bugs me not to be able to use my hands when I want.'

'But you said—'

'Jesus, when will you stop making excuses? Man the fuck up.'

Dan sat straight. A great weariness trickled through his body but he made one last attempt, rolling on to his knees for another tackle. This time Pete didn't even pretend to fight. Dan reeled when Pete pushed him, cracking his head against the gravel. When he tried to get up, he couldn't: Pete sat on him.

Something cold and soft squished beneath his shoulder. 'You have no right—' he began.

'Shut up. Hear what I'm saying. When your sub asked for a sub of her own you gave her your best friend, so you didn't have to watch her choose another man. You thought I was safe and easy, a quick fix to 'scratch an itch.' But it's more than that, isn't it? Karen *needs* this. And you don't want to give it to her.'

He stared into Pete's narrowed eyes, thrown into shadow by the bulk of the house. Yellow light streamed through the window and lit the ground around them.

Then the door to the neighbouring house opened. 'Hey, you two want to take this little scrap somewhere else? My children are trying to sleep; it's a school night.'

'Fuck off,' Dan snapped, a split second before Pete cried, 'Bite me, lady!'

The woman huffed and gasped. 'I'm only saying keep it down.' She slammed the door.

Alone again, Dan glared at his friend. He tried to move, but it cost Pete nothing to hold him in place. More squishiness spread beneath his shoulder and back.

Oh, crap.

'Get off,' he muttered. A horrid smell teased his nostrils.

'Are you going to listen?'

'I'm lying in cat shit, you stupid fucker. Get off me.'

Pete stopped pushing. 'What?'

'Can't you smell it? It's all over this bloody gravel. The woman next door has six of the little shit-machines scratching at the door all hours of the night. You're probably kneeling in it.'

Pete sniffed. Wrinkled his nose. 'Ah, hell's balls.' He stood slowly, inspecting his jeans. Sure enough a smear of something brown and stinking coloured his knees and shin. 'And my washing machine is broken too.'

Dan sat up, tugging at his coat. More of the brown smears dotted his back and shoulders. He groaned. 'I liked this jacket. One of the few things Mum bought me that doesn't look like it belongs to Hugh Hefner.' Still muttering he tugged the jacket off completely, rolled it into a ball and shoved it into the black bin.

Legs apart, hands held off his body, Pete watched him warily. 'Can we talk now? Like grown ups?'

Dan sighed. 'Not until you get cleaned up.'

In the bedroom, Dan fished through drawers while Pete waited behind him, shuffling from foot to foot in his boxers. 'I don't know how much I have that will fit you.'

'Sure,' Pete muttered. 'Rub it in, slim.'

'No, I mean you've got more muscle than me. Most of my trousers will be tight on you. Here.' He dragged an old pair of grey joggers from the bottom of the drawer. 'Try those.'

Sure enough, as Pete wiggled his way into the joggers, he struggled to get the waistband over his thighs. 'Skinny little runt, aren't you?'

Dan dragged off his own jeans and swapped them for a fresh pair. And a shirt for good measure. 'I don't play rugby, that's all. And I have a desk job.' He leaned against the wall, toying with Karen's moisturisers lined up on top of the chest of drawers.

'You could still play.'

'I'm past that now. I should have kept going like you did. Seven years is a long time to be out of the game.'

Pete walked awkwardly across the room and perched on the end of the bed. 'You used to be good. Like a whippet.'

'Good times,' Dan agreed.

'What happened?'

'We got old.'

'*You* got old.'

He shrugged.

Pete traced a pattern on the duvet with his forefinger. 'Dan, I meant what I said. I don't want our friendship to fizzle over this. Seven years and the rest. We owe it to each other to sort this out.'

'You tried to rape my girlfriend.'

'You know that's not true.'

'Fine. You're in love with my girlfriend and mauled her in my back garden. Then you told her father that I hit her, leading him to knock me almost into concussion.'

Pete flinched. 'I would never hurt her. I made a mistake. But as soon as she reacted the way she did, I knew it was wrong. I wanted to apologise then. I would never, ever—'

'I know.' Dan raised his hand. 'I do know that on some level. I'm just so . . .'

'Angry?'

'Yeah.'

'Disappointed?'

'Hell yes.'

'I know.' Pete rocked to his feet and began pacing. 'You hate me, right? Fine: I deserve it. I'm sure there's some friends' code about your best mate's girlfriend, and I stomped all over that.'

'Pete, it's not you I'm angry with.' Dan picked up a bottle of hair oil and rolled it along his palms. It left a strong minty scent on his fingers which immediately brought Karen into the room with him.

He sighed, clenching and unclenching his fingers as he thought about Pete's words outside. About Karen and the munch. About their conversations on subs. Over and over she had tested the waters, saying what she needed in as clear a way as she could. And every time he ignored it. Because it hurt. Because it was risky. Because it was hard.

He put the bottle down. 'It's me. *I* did this.'

Stunned silence from his friend.

'You were right—what you said before about half measures. I hate you, but you're right. This is my fault.'

'Wow.'

'She's out there somewhere. Cindy can't find her and she isn't with any of the other girls. Nobody from the university has seen her and even Robert came here looking for her, so she's not with her parents either. She could be anywhere.'

'Mobile?'

'She's not answering. I've tried.'

'What are you going to do?'

Dan gazed at the carpet. 'Not a damn clue. But she'll come home, right? She has to.'

'Eventually. But I meant about this sub thing.'

'She was talking to some guy at the munch today. And she showed me his profile before you showed up. Black Angelus or something like that.'

Pete just waited.

'She likes him. It's subtle, but I can tell. She never normally gets tongue-tied talking about guys and certainly not about other kinksters. But this Sith, or whatever it was, has her all jumbled up.'

'And you don't like him?'

'I don't know him. I mean, I saw him. He looks a bit like Robert.'

Pete snorted. 'So long as he doesn't try to stamp on your head, he's fine by me.'

'You said you love her. How can you stand it?' He trudged across the small space and stood before his friend. 'How can you stand the thought of another man touching her?'

'I'm used to it. I see it every day, don't I?'

Dan stared at his friend as if seeing him for the first time. 'Oh.'

'She's with you and she's happy. When she sees you her eyes get all shiny and she's got this smile; it lights everything up. Seeing her like that makes me happy too. But that's what counts: *she's* happy. That's how I stand it.'

'I'm sorry, Pete.'

'Don't worry about it. Plenty of other fish in the sea, or whatever bollocks they tell you to make it easier.'

Sighing, Dan crossed his arms. 'Sorry about your face.'

'It's fine. Like I said, you hit like a girl.'

'Screw you, you big jock.'

'Bite me, desk jockey.' Pete mock punched him in the arm.

'Wanker.'

'Pervert.'

Dan grinned.

KAREN

Karen kept walking as Sith called her name. She didn't turn, even when his footsteps pounded after her. When he caught up and grabbed her arm she stopped. But she couldn't look at him.

'Where are you going?' he puffed.

'Home.'

'You told me you live in Evington. That's further than you were planning to walk before.'

'I'll be fine.' She snatched her arm away.

'If you won't let me drive, at least let me give you cab fare. I don't want it to end like this. I'm frustrated, but I'm not cruel. Do you have any idea what time it is?'

Karen faced him. Sith had left his house without a coat. A bright shaft of golden light spilled through his open front door some distance behind. On his feet were two mismatched shoes, one slipper, one shiny shoe of soft, buffed leather. Little puffs of condensation billowed from his lips as he shivered and rubbed his arms.

She gazed deep into his eyes and tried to figure out what to say. To find a way to make things better and wipe the look of hurt away. Nothing came to mind. 'I like you, Sith. We have chemistry. But until I clear up this crap with Dan, I need to stay away from you.'

He opened his mouth but she continued over him. 'You're sweet. Sensitive. Kind. Your body is fucking ridiculous and your need to submit makes me crazy. I want to do things to you that will—' Deep breath. 'But I can't. It's too easy to fall into what I *want* with you, instead of *what's right.*'

'But your relationship is open. You've already said Dan sees other women.'

'He doesn't *see* other women, he tops them.'

'What's the difference?'

'Our sexual dynamic is open but our *relationship* isn't. They're two different things. When he tops other women, he does it *with me.* Sith, this is covert. I haven't spoken with Dan about you properly and when I tried, he was too upset to think straight. Our first rule about other partners is openness and honesty. If I can't do that, then *I'm* the one breaking the rules. *I'm* hurting *him.*'

'But what about your needs?'

Karen pushed her hands into the sleeves of her coat and hunkered down into her collar. 'They'll be dealt with. But by *me,* not you. Goodnight, Sith.' She walked on, leaving him gaping. It should have felt good. Right. Instead Karen sniffed hard, alarmed to find tears gathering in her eyes.

It wasn't fair. How could someone so perfect be so out of reach? And why, despite leaving him, did she feel like a traitor to Dan?

Because I am. I'm a terrible person.

Three streets away she stopped, wiped her eyes and checked her pockets for change. The shrapnel she found was just enough to make bus fare, so she hurried to the next stop on the route towards the city centre. Only after five minutes of waiting did she check the schedule and realise that buses had stopped more than half an hour ago.

Walking it is then. Great.

More than once she considered calling Dan. She thought about asking him to pick her up. He would, she knew that. He'd probably break every speed limit on the way and earn himself a handful of tickets. But he *would* come.

But she wasn't ready for that. Not with her betrayal so close.

How did people do it? How could people stand to cheat on the ones they loved? How did they have the stomach for it? Didn't it make them sick inside?

Even if she did manage to reach home before 2 a.m., Karen knew Dan would be waiting for her. He'd want to talk. She had no idea if she would be able to look him in the eye after what she'd done.

The memory of Sith's hands lingered on her body. She felt his lips against her breasts and the scratch of his stubble as he tongued his way down her stomach. His fingers touched her arms again, teasing over her wrists.

I want a shower.

Her pace quickened, as if by running she could out-manoeuvre the guilt looming overhead. But it followed, dogging every step, no matter how fast she moved.

Her eyes prickled again.

She longed for advice. For a calm, gentle voice to tell her it was okay.

Out came the mobile again. By instinct she scrolled for Cindy's number, but dismissed that idea before clearing the Bs. Next, she thought of her mother. It warmed her for all of two seconds before she remembered Charlaine had her own problems.

The phone flashed on 'Robert Mob.'

Fuck, no. I'm not that desperate.

But there was *one* person. One calm, level headed, mature person who could be more of a father than her own ever managed to be. And by a stroke of luck, he was in the city that night.

But would that be easier than talking to Dan?

As a breath of chilly air swept down the street, buffeting her from side to side, Karen decided it had to be. She scrolled through her numbers and tapped 'Call.'

The phone rang. And rang.

Just as she was about to give up, a little click indicated a connection.

Silence. Then a hushed, 'Hello?'

She took a deep breath. 'Julian? It's Karen.'

'Hello, my dear. Is everything okay? It's quite late, you know.'

'Yes, I'm sorry. Everything's fine.'

The silence at the other end said far more than words ever could.

'Okay, it's not fine. Dan's okay, I'm okay—I mean, we're not hurt—but I need to talk to you.'

A heavy sigh whistled down the phone. 'I was hoping to speak to Dan first. I had no idea this would be so difficult.'

She stopped walking. 'What?'

'Oh, come now, my dear. You don't need to make it easier for me. I know it must be awkward, but I'd like to thank you for taking the first step. You're very brave.'

She shook her head, even though he couldn't see it. 'What are you talking about?'

'When you left today, I knew the jig was up. Then when I got back, Maxine told me Daniel had been ringing and asking about me. The conversation we had before that made it quite clear. But I'm not cheating. I want to make that plain from the offset. Maxine knows exactly what's going on.'

Karen squinted. 'When we left where?'

'The munch, my dear. The munch.'

She gave a squeal. 'You saw us?'

'Hardly difficult with the pair of you flapping like a pair of turkey grouse. I understand you didn't want to be seen, but you weren't very subtle.'

'Shit—I mean, sorry, Julian, but, shit. I didn't know you knew.'

'I didn't until today. And I don't know details—nor do I want to—but I know you and my boy are kinky.'

Karen slumped against a lamppost. The world seemed tipped on its head, spun around, flipped sideways and yanked inside out. After a moment she straightened. 'So are you and Maxine.'

'No.'

'What else would you be doing at a munch? Don't deny it now.'

'I'm not denying, I'm correcting. *I'm* kinky. Maxine is not.' Julian sighed. She could almost picture him, snowy white whiskers fluttering as he did so. He even flicked his hair, the same way Dan did when an overlong strand fell into his eyes. '*I'm* kinky. Maxine has no time for such things. I doubt the woman has a sex drive any more, but I do.'

Shutting her eyes did nothing to drive the image from her mind, but Karen did it anyway. 'I don't want to know.'

'Nor should you. But you deserve the truth. And clearly Dan needs it too since he's worried about cheating. Thank you again for doing this. It's brave of you to try fixing matters.'

Now the moment had come Karen barely knew what to do. She scuffed her foot against the pavement, working the sticky edge of a flattened pat of gum.

Is this better, or worse?

Somehow, revealing her infidelity to another kinkster was that much harder. 'I didn't call for him.'

A lone car drove by. Karen squinted into the light then returned to staring at her shoes.

'What's the matter, dear?'

'I cheated on Dan.' The words were a whisper, almost lost in the wind. But he heard them. She knew he did because of his sharp intake of breath.

'When?'

'Just now. Half an hour ago. I'm not even sure. I went to another man's house. Not on purpose—he picked me up— ugh! This is coming out wrong.'

'Why don't you start at the beginning?'

She sniffed. 'I met a man at the munch today. His name is Sith.'

'Tall? Good looking? Dreadlocks like your father?'

A wince. 'Please don't compare him to Robert. Not after what we just did.'

'Sorry. Please continue.'

Karen bit her lip. 'We talked about what we wanted from our relationships. Dan and I are D/s but I want more than that. I need to try other things and Sith was perfect. He *is* perfect.'

Julian seemed to be thinking. When he spoke again it was hushed and chased by the sound of him moving through a small space. 'So you had relations with him?'

'No! I just dominated him a bit. And let him do the same to me. But it didn't feel right. The whole time, even when I knew it's what I wanted, I knew it wasn't right. I can't do it without Dan there. I need him.' Tears rolled freely down her cheeks. 'What have I done?'

'Karen, dear, calm down. Let me just move to a more private spot. One moment.' More rustling, then the sound of muted footsteps. When Julian next spoke, he did so at his normal volume. 'There now. Better. Are you okay?'

'Not really. I've done something terrible. You heard him on the phone today, he despises cheaters. So do I. Like my dad.' She gave a whimper. 'I've turned into Robert.'

'I doubt that very much. You are far too kind, generous and, dare I say it, well spoken to be anything like that man. And you have your mother's looks.'

'Thank you.'

He chuckled. 'Now that you're calmer, let me tell you something. When I told Maxine I wanted to explore kink, she spent three hours lecturing me about sodomites, paedophiles and rapists. When she eventually calmed down, I told her that all I wanted was the occasional bit of bondage. A chance to let a woman have her way with me.'

Karen cringed. 'Julian, I—'

'Do you know what she told me?'

'I could make some pretty good guesses.'

Another laugh. 'She told me that I could do whatever I wanted, so long as I told her about it first. She said that her sex drive had been low for years and she didn't miss it. There were 'more important' things to do. But if I needed something that she couldn't provide, she was happy for me to find it so long as I did it honestly and safely.'

Yet again Karen leaned against the lamppost. She shook her head. 'Seriously?'

'Yes. Well, maybe not those exact words, but you know Maxine. But her main concern was safety. None of this—now how did she put it? No 'crawling the pavement for skinny hookers with bad make up and worse dye jobs.''

Karen snorted through her tears. 'Yes, that sounds like Maxine.'

'I don't know what sort of arrangement you have with my son, but he loves you. I'm sure if you talk to him he'll understand you made a mistake.'

'But it's more than that. I need something he can't—or won't—give me. He tried.' She shuddered at the thought of Pete in that ridiculous mask. 'It was a disaster.'

'But he did *try*. Love means a lot of things, Karen, but something most people agree on is wanting the person you love to be happy.'

'Happy doesn't mean cheating.'

'You made a mistake. But it sounds like you stopped yourself from making a much larger mistake. You knew what was right, what wasn't and you made the right choice. That has to count for something.'

'I hope so.'

'Talk to Daniel. I know it's late but he'll want to discuss this. Do it before it gets any later.'

She sniffed. 'I can't.'

'I know you're scared but you're a strong, young woman.'

Though the sentiment made her smile, the facts were unchanged. 'No, I really can't. I'm miles from home. No money. I really don't want to have this conversation with Dan on the way home. I can't call him.'

'Come here then.'

'I can't, remember. No money.'

'Get the cab to come here and I will give you the fare. Then travel the rest of the way home.'

'I couldn't do that.'

'Do you plan to walk home?'

Karen tucked her free hand into the sleeve of her jacket. 'I'd rather not.'

'So flag down the first cab you see and direct it to our hotel. I'll meet you outside.'

Before she could stop them, tears of frustration and worry shifted into sobs of relief. 'Thank you so much, Julian. I don't know what to say.'

'Don't say anything. Just call Dan and let him know you're coming home.'

'I will.'

'And don't tell him about the munch, please.'

'You prefer to let him think you're cheating?'

'I'll talk to him later, on my own terms. Will you do that for me, my dear? Let me decide how and when to talk to him.'

'Of course.'

'Thank you. See you in a short while.' He hung up.

For long moments Karen held the mobile, deciding what to say. In the end she gave up and scrolled through her numbers to find Dan's.

He answered after two rings.

'Where the hell are you? If you don't turn up soon Cindy is going to turn my nuts into a pair of maracas.'

She laughed, even as tears trickled down her face. 'I forgot I'd called her.'

'Where are you?'

'Coming home. I'll be there soon.'

'I'll be waiting.'

'Good. I love you.'

Dan hesitated. 'I love you, too.' Relief was clear in his voice. 'Please let Cindy know you're okay.'

'I will.' Smiling, Karen hung up, tucked the phone into her pocket and marched towards the nearest taxi rank.

DAN

Dan spent several minutes pacing the living room. Every headlight flashing across the windows made him twitch aside the curtains, scanning for Karen climbing from a cab. When she finally appeared at the end of the road, a little tension eased from his shoulders. It landed in his back and stomach, which clenched as he thought about the long and potentially painful conversation they were about to have.

But we have to.

He rushed to the door and threw it open. Karen paused at the end of the garden path, eyes wide. He trailed a finger along the door frame. 'I'm sorry,' he whispered.

She fussed with a lock of her hair. 'Me too.'

'Pete was a stupid idea. I know that now. I guess I knew it at the time, but I panicked. I can't stand the thought of not giving you what you need.'

'Even if what I need is another man?' Her voice was low, gaze downcast. She shifted from fiddling with her hair to the buttons on her jacket.

He hesitated.

'Let's go inside.'

She walked into the house, patting his shoulder as she passed.

Dan shut the door.

In the living room, Karen peeled off her coat and toed off her shoes. She sat rigid, hands planted on her knees. Her left leg stuttered, heel drumming the floor. After a few taps she seemed to realise what she was doing. The taps stopped. She looked up, brown eyes wide and sincere. 'I met Sith tonight.'

'Black Angelus?'

She nodded.

Through a stab of anger, Dan spoke as softly as he could. 'Right.' Not enough. Not nearly enough for the whirlwind in his mind. He shoved it to one side.

Stay calm.

Buying time, Dan inched into the living room and sat on the end of the sofa. He ran his hands through his hair and scratched the trail of stubble across his neck and jaw. 'You went out to meet him?'

'I went to Cindy's first. She wasn't there.'

'Helsinki.'

'Ah.' Karen rolled her eyes. 'Of course; where else would she be on a Sunday night?'

'You know her better than I do.'

A shrug. Then, 'Sith took me there first, then realised I couldn't get anywhere else.'

'He has your number?' More anger seeped through. With effort, Dan tamped it down.

'After we fought, I talked to him on *Kink4Life*. We exchanged numbers.' She gazed at him, calm and steady.

'So, instead of coming home so we could talk, you went off with this guy?'

So much for staying calm.

'To his house.'

He froze. 'Kaz, I don't get what you're doing. Are you *trying* to make me angry? Or jealous? Because it's really working. You met this guy *today* and then you went to his house?'

'And let him touch me.'

He couldn't see. Couldn't think. Couldn't breathe passed the thick sensation of nausea crawling up his throat. Not anger. Not any more. No space for that. 'What the hell?'

Karen's rigid control broke. She threw herself to the ground so hard the impact rocked through her body and made her teeth knock together. It didn't stop her. She crawled across the carpet until near enough to touch the tips of her fingers against his instep. 'I'm so sorry.'

'Karen, get up.'

'No, I—I need you to know I'm sorry.'

He tugged his toes away from her fingers. 'Fine. But don't crawl around on the floor, we're not doing that now. Talk to me.' When she continued to avoid his gaze, he hauled her up himself. She flinched beneath his grip, then twisted away.

When she spoke, she spoke to his chest. 'I let him touch me. I was so upset—I wanted someone to hold me. I wanted you and your strength and your control.'

'Kaz.'

'I was too angry! I didn't want *you*, but I wanted what you *do*. You always make the hard stuff easier. You make me forget. I wanted that.'

He shook his head. 'I don't know what you're trying to say.'

'I let him touch me like you do. I submitted.' Her words dissolved into a trembling sigh. More tears cascaded down her cheeks and gathered on her chin before beginning their free fall. Then she stopped. Brushed her face. Looked him in the eye. 'I wanted a master in that moment and it wasn't you.' She slid back to her knees and put her hands on her thighs, palm up. 'But that wasn't enough. I made him submit to me too.'

A giant fist reached inside Dan's chest and clawed his heart out. He lurched forward, stunned at how breathless he felt. How weak. How sick.

Karen knelt at his feet, that submissive pose she used so well to mock him only a few hours ago.

What to do? What *could* he do? Shout? Scream? Walk out? So many options. So much pain. Chest-crunching, heart-wringing pain.

Dan sat on the armchair, his fingernails scoring deep grooves in the leather. Several attempts to moisten his lips finally left him able to speak. 'Did you like it?' The words cost him everything.

'Yes.' Her gazed locked on his and Dan realised then that she wasn't crying. Her eyes were bright, yes, but tears no longer streaked her cheeks. Her mouth formed a thin line, the muscles of her jaw knotted and tight. 'It felt wonderful,

Dan. Everything I wanted right there and willing, but I couldn't do it.'

'Why?'

'Because I'm *your sub*. I might be your girlfriend, but first I was your submissive. That means more to me than anything.'

'And Black Angelus?' He managed to speak the name with less venom than usual, even as his mind fed him the image of grabbing those thick dreadlocks and yanking them free of the roots.

'He's gorgeous and sexy and willing . . . and none of that matters. I can't act on anything without permission.'

'Whose?'

'Yours.' Before the word was fully free of her mouth she shook her head. 'My master's permission.'

Too much. None of it made sense. He rubbed his face with both hands. 'Get up, Kaz. I can't think with you down there.'

'No.'

He glared at her. 'Get up!'

'No, Sir.' Her gaze hardened. 'I betrayed you and your trust. We need to deal with that first.'

Only then did he understand what was happening. The brutal honesty. The submissive postures and downcast eyes. He remembered such actions from the early days of their relationship, when love was a distant myth and they met twice a week to scratch their kinky itches. Pure D/s. Nothing else.

'Karen,' he began.

'Sir, please,' she bit her lip. 'I know I shouldn't ask, but please? Can we settle this first?'

He frowned. 'But you're more than a sub now. You're not Hannah or Rebecca. I love you.'

Her lower lip wobbled. 'Please?'

A heavy sigh flowed from his lips. He longed to resist, but her earlier words echoed in his mind, accusing him of hiding behind his master role when things got tough. Why should she be any different with her submissive role? But it was a gamble. A big one.

He sat straighter in the chair. 'Fine. Is that what you want now?'

'I—' she hesitated. 'I don't know.'

'Permission. That's what you said you needed. Is that why you're here?'

She flinched. A flicker of uncertainty entered her gaze.

'Well?' he snapped. Another flinch. Dan swept off the chair in one quick move, walking around so she could no longer see his face. More importantly, so he could no longer see hers. 'What do you want, Karen?'

Her shoulders hunched. 'I want you to make it better. I want you to believe I'm sorry. I want . . .'

He shook his head. She couldn't see, but it didn't matter. If that was what she really wanted he could do it. *Would* do it.

No more half measures.

'Stand up.'

Scrabbling to meet the order, Karen rushed to her feet. When she faced him, he cut her off.

'Go over there. Link your wrists above your head and rest them on the wall.'

A fraction of hesitation, then she obeyed, facing out. Hope brightened her features, not quite relief, but certainly not the unchecked misery of moments ago.

Again, Dan shook his head. No way could he do this if he could see her face. 'Turn around.'

She stiffened, head to toe. Fighting with her natural instinct to fight him. The nerves of 'every day Karen' battled with the needs of 'submissive Karen'. Fight shone in her eyes. The struggle tightened her jaw, made her chest heave.

He waited. It was all he could do.

When she finally turned to face the wall, Dan's chest loosened. The fist squeezing his heart and lungs relinquished its hold and allowed him to breathe.

Maybe this *was* the right way. What they *both* needed to move on from this mess.

He approached, careful to make his footfalls heavy.

With each step, she stiffened further until he feared her body might crumble from the pressure. He touched her shoulder. Trailed his fingers across the back of her neck then down her spine.

'As my girlfriend you've hurt me. As my sub . . . betrayal isn't strong enough a word. You've disappointed me so much. We have rules.' He had to stop. Moisten his lips again. 'We have those rules for a reason. We agreed them together so no one would get hurt. You broke the rules and now I'm hurting.'

'I'm sorry—'

'No! No talking. You listen. It's not that you let someone else touch you, though that kills me. It's that you hid it. You didn't wait for permission or follow any of the rules designed to keep us both safe.'

Karen sagged against the wall. She didn't speak, but every tense muscle in her body gave away the truth. She was listening and she agreed.

'I don't want you to ask for anything.' He gritted his teeth. 'You're mine. You want me to let another man touch you and that is a big deal. It's not like the Slave Library. It doesn't compare. *You* are *mine*.' He smacked the flat of his palm against her arse. 'Letting another man touch you is a big fucking deal.' Another swat of her butt, this time using both hands to stroke her hips.

She relaxed. A tiny bit.

Not good.

When he spanked her again, he put all his weight behind it, slamming his palm against her arse so hard his fingers became numb.

She yelped, but said nothing.

Dan unfastened her jeans and pulled them down to her ankles. Her underwear, he pulled as far as her knees. Damp. Musky. Seeing it rekindled the rage, wafting the sparks with fans of jealousy.

'Did he do this? Make you wet? Answer me!'

'Yes.'

The knowledge that another man had been there gave him a physical ache. 'How? What did he do?'

'He . . .' she whimpered.

'Tell me.'

'He told me what he would do if he were the master and there was another sub under me. He kissed my breasts.'

The whole time she spoke, Dan caressed her bare rear. Each time he thought rage might consume him, he smacked her cheeks. Her skin grew warm beneath his palm. 'Is that all?'

'No.'

Another smack. 'Then keep going.'

'I pulled his t-shirt over his face so he couldn't see. I made him put his hands behind his head and wait. And I kissed his stomach.'

'And?' Smack.

'I wanted to pull his trousers down. See his cock. I wanted to touch it. Lick it. Make him beg.'

'Did you?' Smack, smack.

'No.'

Tears now. He saw them. Heard them. When they fell, they soaked into her blouse and left tiny damp patches in their wake.

He spanked her again. 'Why not?'

'I couldn't. I needed you. It doesn't matter if I want a sub or not, even if I get one, I can't enjoy it knowing you're unhappy. Or that you don't know about it. I don't want to hurt you.'

Dan stepped in until her bare rear pressed into his crotch. He thrust against her, making sure she could feel there was nothing straining through his trousers. His head was clear, his thoughts crystal.

'I want to hurt you,' he murmured in her ear. 'I want to spank you until you're crying, begging me to stop. I'm hurt, Kaz. And *so* angry. I want to spank you until your backside glows with the heat of it and you can't sit down. And I'm frustrated as hell because I could never do that to you. I could never *actually* hurt you no matter what you do to me. Besides, no physical pain can match what's going on in my head right now.'

She lowered her head to the wall. 'Then try, Sir.'

'Pardon?'

'Do it. Punish me.'

Dan shoved back from her body so hard he stumbled. 'No.'

'Yes, Sir. Punish me. That gives us a clean slate.'

'Don't be silly. We don't do that.'

'We've never had to. But this will be a lesson for both of us. Punish me.'

Karen turned. Her wrists remained in place as she swivelled, shuffling with her jeans around her ankles. 'It's

BDSM, Sir. Bondage and discipline. Dominance and submission. Sado-masochism. Masters discipline their subs.' That determined set returned to her jaw along with a sparkle in her eyes that had nothing to do with tears but the fierce independent streak that made her such an unpredictable submissive. 'When we began, we promised honesty and openness. I betrayed that today.'

'You were upset.'

'That's no excuse,' she snapped. 'It's like the woman who says 'I was drunk, I didn't mean to sleep with those thirty men.' It's bullshit. Being drunk frees you, it doesn't make you an idiot or turn you into someone you're not. It makes you *more* like who you are. Same with being angry. Or scared. Or upset.' She stepped forward, shuffling her dropped jeans across the floor. 'I stepped out behind your back and I did it knowingly. Punish me.'

Dan cupped her cheek with a trembling hand. 'I don't want to hurt you. I'm angry, but we can work this out.'

'We can,' she agreed. 'After this.'

He stepped back. On some level she was right, he knew that. But old memories made it difficult to accept. His mouth was suddenly dry, his shoulders hunched. 'I don't know if I can.'

Her gaze softened. 'I'm not Beth. I know my limits. More importantly, *you* know my limits.'

'But—'

'I trust you, Sir.' That said, she turned, linked her wrists and placed them on the wall again. With a flex of her stomach she bent forward, sticking her arse out towards him until her back was parallel to the ground, arms stretched above her head.

It looked uncomfortable. And sexy.

Dan bit his lip and touched her back. She shivered, but said nothing.

'I'll punish you,' he whispered. 'And just like any good punishment, once it's over, the matter is done. I punish you, you accept it, we move on. Understand?'

'Yes, Sir.' The relief in her voice gave him strength to continue.

'Good. How many times did you kiss him?'

'I don't know.'

He grunted and dragged his fingernails over her back. 'You'd better remember Kaz, because it's going to be important.'

'Um . . . about five?'

'*About* five?'

'Okay six.'

'Good. How many times did he kiss your breasts. No, *my* breasts?'

She gasped. 'Lots—he wouldn't stop. He touched them and kissed them and—'

'Fine. We'll guess that too. How many?'

'Ten?'

'Let's go with that. It's a good, round number. ' He stopped stroking her skin long enough to clear his throat. When he spoke again, it was the voice he used in the bedroom, the one that demanded instant obedience and expected nothing less. 'Wait there. Don't move.'

'Okay.'

'Excuse me?' he snarled. Part of him still screamed in terror, but if he wanted to do this at all, it had to be done right.

'I mean, yes, Sir.'

'Damn right. I'll be back.' He left her there, bent over, hands braced against the wall.

Dan aimed for the draining board as he entered the kitchen, his fingers stroking over plates, cups and dishes before finding what he wanted. Picking it up, he carried the tool back to the living room. At the door he paused, hiding out of sight of Karen's awkward position.

She hadn't moved. Not an inch.

Once or twice her fingers flexed. A bead of sweat trickled down the side of her face and vanished into the crack of her lips. He saw her tongue flick out to lap it up.

God, I hope I can do this.

Though he said nothing, he knew she could tell he was back. Her entire body stiffened, every limb singing with fresh tension as he walked around her. When in range, he touched her back again. 'I'm going to spank you with my hand ten times. One for each of Sith's unauthorised kisses. You will count them.'

148

'Yes, Sir.' Karen trembled beneath him. Her skin grew warm beneath his fingers while her knees quaked as she fought to hold her position.

'Then, I'll use this.' As he spoke, Dan positioned himself on her left side so she could see the tool he held.

Her eyes widened. 'Seriously?'

'Yes, Kaz. We don't have a crop and whips draw blood if not used carefully. I've not had enough practise and you're right; I know your limits. I don't want you to bleed, but I *do* want you to feel you've been punished sufficiently for what you've done. So I'll use this.'

'A wooden spoon.' Her voice was a shadow of itself. Then she rallied. Nodded. That gleam returned to her eyes. 'I'm ready, Sir.'

'Count. If you lose count, we start again. Move, we start again. If we get to the spoon and you lose count, we start again. Move, we'll start again from the beginning with my hand. Understand?'

She whimpered. 'Yes. Sir.'

'Good. Get ready.'

Dan faced outward with his hip pressed tight to hers, right arm wrapped around her waist. He used the left hand to touch her exposed cheeks, stroking each one in slow, teasing circles. Each time his hands slowed, her thighs trembled and the muscles in her stomach bunched tight as she tensed for the blow.

When he smacked her, she shrieked and bucked against his grip.

His fingers tingled. His palm numbed. He waited.

'One. Thank you, Sir.'

The thanks was an unexpected touch, but unsurprising. If Dan hadn't already understood this punishment was more for her than him, it might have worried him. But he knew what he had to do. This was the only way to help her move on from what she saw as an unforgivable betrayal.

And yet she hasn't said a word about Pete. I don't deserve this woman.

He spanked her again.

'Two. Thank you, Sir.'

By the eighth slap, Dan could no longer feel his fingers. He saw his hand rise and fall, but aside from the sharp crack of flesh on flesh, he barely knew it was happening.

Karen sobbed openly, shaking on trembling legs.

He braced himself, ready to take her weight if she fell, simultaneously fascinated and proud that she refused to lean against him.

Smack.

'Oh, fuck, fuck, nine! Thank you, Sir.'

He bit his lip. Guilt swelled within him. 'You're doing really well, Karen. Last one. Ready?'

She didn't answer, simply whimpered and thrust out her backside, that was redder than he'd ever known her skin could go.

Smack.

'Ten! Thank you, Sir.'

The sound of her breathing filled the room. Hard and harsh in the ringing silence following the absence of slaps.

Dan forced himself to pick up the spoon. He took several deep breaths to steady his own heart and to let her recover.

She stopped twitching. The whimpers faded. A light tap against the small of her back brought her back to attention.

'Ready?' he murmured.

'Yes, Sir. Do you want me to continue counting or start from 'one' to honour the new tool?'

He smiled. Typical Karen.

'Start from one.'

'Yes, Sir.'

The words barely left her mouth before he brought the head of the spoon down on her rear. He aimed for the meatiest part he could find, but she still jerked against him and bounced on her toes.

'Fuck, shit, fuck! Fuck! One. Thank you, Sir.'

He lifted the spoon. Brought it down.

'Two, thank you, Sir.' Her legs trembled. For brief instants she sagged against his grip before righting herself.

Dan's resolve wavered. 'Tell me your safe words.'

'I don't need them.'

'Do as you're told!'

She straightened her legs. Made fists. 'Take a break, orange. Stop, red.'

He relaxed, but not much.

'I'm okay, Sir. Please, let's finish this.'

Smack. Smack. Smack.

She screamed, dancing on her toes for several seconds. 'Three, four, five. Thank you, Sir.'

Dan's eyes tingled. He wouldn't cry, but he wanted to. The heat coming off Karen's body made his own back sweat. She trembled against his side, a constant hum of motion as she fought to hold her position.

'I can't do it, Kaz. Look at you. I can't.'

'You can,' she whispered.

Despite his own reservations, Dan knew they had to finish. It was the only way. She would never forgive herself if she failed to take her punishment. With his arm tight around her waist, his hip braced against hers, Dan felt every shiver, ever tremor, every shudder. He looked at his handy work and saw faint ridges across her cheeks where the spoon had raised flesh.

He waited. Watching her hands for a sign, listening for a safe word. Neither came.

Nodding he slammed the spoon against her arse. The crack split the air. Her shriek followed.

Dan threw the spoon across the room. He heard a crash but didn't care where it landed.

While Karen sobbed and burbled 'six' over and over again, he turned and took her by the shoulders, slowly lifting her into a standing position. She shrieked again, the change in position bringing a fresh round of tears to her eyes.

He wiped them away with his thumb.

'I'm sorry Dan, I'm sorry. I'm so, sorry. I don't want to cheat on you, I never did—I couldn't—'

'I know, Kaz.' Fighting his own tears, he gathered her into his arms and let her cry against his shoulder. 'It's done now. We don't need to talk about it any more, okay?'

'I love you.'

'I love you, too.'

Karen faced him, eyes red and puffy, cheeks tear stained. A small bubble of saliva pooled in the corner of her mouth.

Never had Dan seen her look so beautiful.

Gripping her chin, he held her in place and pressed a kiss against those full, sweet lips. 'You were amazing. You *are* amazing.'

'I didn't do anything.'

He shook his head. 'Let's go sort out those welts.'

After she kicked off her jeans and knickers, Dan swept her into his arms. Though gentle, he sensed her discomfort and took her straight to the bedroom. 'Lie on your stomach. I'll run the bath.'

He filled the tub with lavender bath oil and a handful of salts. Thinking about it more, he grabbed a handful of candles and shut off the light. When he returned to the bedroom Karen lifted a bleary eye toward him. 'What are you doing?'

He sat beside her. 'I'm your Master. It's my job to take care of you.'

'I know. Thanks. The bath smells wonderful.'

'Not just that.' He checked her rear cheeks for broken skin as he spoke. 'I'm talking about *all* your needs. Even the ones I don't like.'

She sucked in a sharp breath.

'I made a mistake tonight. I thought Pete would be the answer. He's a man, he's our friend, he's safe. But he's not what you want. And after tonight I don't want you to want him. He loves you too, Kaz. I can't believe I didn't see that before, but he does. And I'm sorry I put you through that.'

'It's okay.'

He gave her a steady look.

'Fine, it's not, but you were trying.'

'I need to try harder. No more half measures.' Before she could question the comment he pressed on. 'Tomorrow I want you to call Sith and invite him over.'

Karen flipped on to her back. It must have hurt like a bitch, but she didn't even flinch. 'Seriously?'

'Yes. I want to talk to him. If that's who you want, fine, but I want to meet him first.'

'You don't have to do this.'

'I know. But I choose to. I want you to have everything you need. I want us both to be happy.'

Once more she looked ready to argue. Then an expression of peace and calm crossed her face. 'Thank you.'

'We need to talk about your dad too. You should call him.'

She stiffened. 'I thought the punishment was over?'

'I'm serious. He came here looking for you. I think he really wants to make things right. For your mum.'

Karen stared at the opposite wall for a moment. Sighed. 'I'll call him in the morning.'

'Good girl.' Smiling, Dan took her hand and helped her off the bed. When she stumbled against him, Dan picked her up once more and carried her into the bathroom.

KAREN

Karen bit into another slice of toast and relished the soft ooze of butter through her teeth. She grinned and thumbed a drop off the end of her chin. 'This is nice.'

Dan looked up from his laptop. 'Good.'

'Now I know why *you* like it so much.'

He glanced at her feet, then back up again. Grinned. 'Don't get any ideas.'

'I won't. Believe me, I'm happy like this. Are *you* happy?' She directed the question at the figure on the ground. The hands against her instep paused their motions. 'I didn't say stop.'

The massage resumed. Slow. Sensual. Teasing every nerve ending until her entire body tingled with pleasure. It shot through every limb, every scrap of skin. She moaned, long and low.

Sith lowered his head before he spoke, careful not to look above knee height. 'I'm very happy, Ma'am.'

Karen bent low enough to tuck a butter-greasy finger beneath his chin. When he met her gaze, she smiled at him. 'Glad to hear it.'

He grinned. 'How are your feet, Ma'am?'

'Wonderful.' Another flex of her legs and a cat-like stretch. 'Are you sure you're a barrister? More like a masseuse.'

'I did six months of training in homoeopathy when I finished university.'

'Man of many talents, aren't you? Care you show me what else you can do with those hands?' She groaned as he tucked one long finger between her toes.

'Hell yes! I mean, yes please, Ma'am.'

Karen laughed. Tugging her feet free, she leaned down and dropped a gentle kiss on his forehead. 'Never hide your enthusiasm, Sith. Ever. I want to know how excited you are. It makes me so wet you'd never believe me until I showed you.'

From behind his laptop, Dan cleared his throat.

'Sir, I'm taking Sith upstairs now. Is that okay?'

'Yes. Now tell me the rules.'

She rolled her eyes. 'No coming unless you're there to watch.'

He arched an eyebrow.

'Fine, *I'm* not allowed to come unless you're there to watch. *He's* not allowed to come until *you* say so.'

'Good. Sith, you may come. *If* she lets you.'

'Thank you, Sir.' Sith scrabbled to his feet, stumbling when the chains linking his ankles drew taunt and shortened his stride. 'Thank you.'

Dan gave a dismissive flap of his hand. 'Yeah, yeah. Go on. I'll be there in a few minutes.'

He said it so casually that Karen nearly missed his meaning. Sith froze beside her and stared, mouth hanging slightly open. Karen swallowed and licked her abruptly dry lips. 'You'll what?'

'You heard me. I'm joining you today.'

'But you've never . . .'

'I know. It's about time I did.' Dan leaned back, tipping his chair to balance on the rear legs. 'I should be used to the idea by now.'

Sith gave a cry somewhere between a shriek and a whimper of joy. 'What are you going to do?'

'No idea. I'll figure it out later. But first, these reports.'

Karen gave a cry of her own, lust mingled with excitement and terror. 'Dan, I—'

He cleared his throat again.

'Sir, I know I've been talking about it, but you don't have to.'

'Ha,' he let the chair thump back into place. 'It's not about you, Kaz. Maybe I want to see how well we double team you.'

Oh, fuck . . .

Her body responded with a flush of heat that billowed down and flooded the junction between her legs. 'Double team?'

A smirk. 'Go on, Sith. Warm her up for me.'

'Yes, Sir!' He scrambled off his knees, adjusting himself within a tiny, lacy thong.

Spying his discomfort, Karen touched his cheek. 'Don't worry. I'll get that off you as soon as we're upstairs. If I knew you'd like it so much I would have made you wear it longer.'

He flushed. 'I don't normally wear women's underwear. But it's yours—and you already made it so wet—'

'I understand. Come on.' She clipped a lead to the big loop protruding from the plain, black collar around his neck. She led him up the stairs, moving slow to make sure he didn't trip on the chains.

In the bedroom with the lights dimmed and the door closed, an unnatural twilight fell on the room.

'Strip me.' Though she tried to make the demand authoritative, Karen couldn't keep the giddy glee from her voice. It never got old. Even after three weeks.

Sith moved closer, his body a dark smudge in the dim light. As her eyes adjusted, she saw the gleam of silver about his ankles and the soft, tartan slippers he wore to ward off the chill of the laminate floor.

Slippers and chains. What an excellent combination.

Sith's hands trembled when they touched her. She held her breath.

He handled her as though she were a delicate sculpture of spun glass, one that might crack or splinter if used too roughly. First the corset, unlacing the ribbons at the back while breathing softly into her ear.

'Tell me what you're thinking,' she murmured.

'I'm thinking about how lucky I am, Ma'am. That I can't believe I'm here with you. This is the most incredible—'

'No. What are you *thinking*.'

He paused. 'I want to feel your tits. I want to touch your nipples and wet them with my tongue. I want to see your body as I unwrap it like a present. I want to fuck you.' His breathing quickened. 'I want to feel your hot cunt juice all over my face and taste it as you ride my mouth.'

She gasped, grinding her thighs together. 'That's more like it.'

The corset loosened. She stretched and exhaled deeper than she had for the past two hours. The leather slid away from her body and her skin prickled in the cool air. Her nipples stood to immediate attention.

Sith groaned.

'Touch them,' she ordered.

He did, at once, gripping her breasts with both hands and squeezing so tight it ached. When she pushed back against him, the thong he wore did nothing to hide his erection. He pressed against her rear. Hot and so, so ready.

'Good. Now the skirt.'

His hands lingered on her breasts before beginning the journey down. His strong hands skimmed her ribs, hips, then caught on the waistband of her skirt. He eased it down slow enough to tease them both. As the fabric inched over her thighs, Karen became aware of the slippery dampness between them.

The skirt hit the floor with a soft 'whumph.'

She faced him.

His eyes widened as he saw her thighs. 'Sweet Jesus. How long have you been wearing that?'

'Since before you arrived. Why do you think the thong was so wet?'

As if on cue, Karen jerked forward with a low moan. The bullet wedged inside her gave a long, throbbing hum, vibrating at an intensity high enough to make the protruding antennae tremble between her thighs.

Sith caught her by the arms and held her steady. 'What's wrong?'

'It's on. He turned it on.'

'Dan did? It's remote controlled?'

Karen managed a sly smile while fighting rising waves of pleasure. 'You're *my* sub, Sith, but I'm *his*. He's always going to be in charge.'

Laughing, Sith clapped his hands together and raised them towards the ceiling, faking a gesture of prayer. 'I love being part of your life, Karen.'

She gave him a two handed shove, giggling as he peddled his arms to save himself. The chains wouldn't let him and he tumbled back onto the bed.

'Wait a second—'

But she didn't wait. She leapt onto his chest and sat there, pinning his arms with her knees. 'Now . . . what was it you called me?'

He finally caught on. 'Sorry, I meant, Ma'am. Ma'am!'

'Too late.' Snatching a crop from the bed, she reached back and started swatting his thighs and shins.

He yelped and squealed and jerked around, but she leaned into him, squeezing his arms in place. The whole time her slit rubbed against his chest, slicking him up, while the vibrating bullet wedged inside her buzzed its pleasure song.

'Please, Ma'am, please, please.'

She paused. 'Yes?'

'Let me make it up to you.'

'You're such a good boy. Go on then.'

Karen picked up a square packet of red foil and tore it with her teeth. The little sheet of latex flopped out and she pressed it against her pussy before wriggling her way up his body, shuffling up until her slit hovered above his open mouth. He licked his lips. Put out his tongue.

'Make it good, Sith.'

Within minutes Karen found herself battling to hold off one of the most intense orgasms of her life. Sith's tongue danced around her swollen lips, back and forth, up and down. First soft, then hard, fast, then slow. He teased her, never once settling on a rhythm that might let her work toward a true orgasm. Each time her thighs shuddered around his head, he pulled back, puffing air on her damp flesh until the dual sensations of hot and cold made her curse.

She reached back again with the crop, studding his thighs and crotch with light strokes. Each time the heart shaped head struck the front of those lacy knickers he groaned and thrust his tongue into her creamy core.

The bullet stopped buzzing.

Karen jerked her head up, dazed. In the half dark, she glimpsed the outline of Sith's stunned features before a voice from behind sent a shudder racing up and down her spine.

'Having fun, Kaz?'

She hadn't even heard him come in.

Dan stood near the door, the remote for the bullet held at hip height. With deliberate, slow motions, he raised his thumb, then lowered it, pushing a button near the top of the remote. The bullet picked up with a slow, rolling ebb of vibrations, enough to be noticed but not much more.

'I asked you a question, Kaz.'

'Yes, Sir.' The words stuck to her tongue. She had to swallow twice to get them out. 'I'm having fun.'

'Good. Then stop.'

Though she knew it was coming, the rush of disappointment was so strong she almost cried. Though she took as long as she dared, Karen raised her slit from Sith's mouth and pulled the dental dam away.

Sith looked like he'd lost his favourite present.

She stood near the side of the bed, folding the square of latex into a small bundle that she dropped into the bin near the chest of drawers.

'Good girl.'

Dan's praise made the loss worth while.

She stared at his face, and even in the dim light, Karen found pride there. Love. Raw, animal lust.

'Come here.'

Dignity and pride had no place. Karen ran to him, bobbing to her knees when in range. At this height the bulge in his trousers was clear. 'May I suck you, Sir?' she whispered.

'God no,' he laughed. 'I'm so horny I'd burst through your throat. I'm going to fuck you.'

A thrill of pleasure burst in her belly and fanned outward, lighting every limb with the flame of lust. 'What shall I—I mean how—'

He saved her from finding a way to ask the awkward question by putting out his hand. She took it and stood. 'Sith, off the bed.'

'Yes, Sir.' The other man moved for Dan's command in a way he never quite managed for hers.

Karen couldn't help but notice the way his erection continued to fight for freedom, not at all daunted by the third party. If anything, he looked delighted to see Dan there. She shared the sentiment. Dan's involvement was more than she ever hoped for and she shivered, overcome. Her hands fluttered as excitement got the better of her. 'Sir?'

He raised a hand to silence her. Looked at Sith. 'Sit on the floor at the end of the bed, legs out, hands behind your head.'

When Sith looked her way, Karen was ready for it. She pointed. 'You heard him. Hop to it.'

He smiled, sat on the floor, laced his fingers and put them behind his head.

'Good boy,' she murmured, squeezing her thighs together. Dan's hand against her hip reminded her of his presence. 'And me, Sir?'

'Stand with your feet on either side of his knees. Bend forward and brace your hands against the end of the bed.'

When she took the position described, Sith craned his head back to gaze at her, eyes wide and round. She kissed his forehead, grinning when his hands twitched. He wanted to touch her; his need burned hot and bright in his eyes.

'Keep your hands where they are,' she said. 'Master didn't say anything about touching.'

He groaned, long and deep from the back of his throat. One knee twitched to press against her foot.

His submission thrilled her. Gave her a sense of control and authority. She could do anything. Ask for anything. Say anything. Her mouth opened. She planned to tease him, to order that he watch but not touch. Then Dan arrived behind her and blotted out everything else.

His hand stroked down her spine, a firm, commanding touch that left her shuddering. While one hand massaged her breasts, the other teased up the inside of her thigh and tugged on the bullet still humming inside her.

'Time to fill you up with something else, Kaz.'

She locked gazes with Sith. 'Yes, please, Sir. I'm ready.'

The bullet slid from her body. She didn't see where it landed, just heard it hit the floor and roll away. The sudden emptiness left her moaning, twitching. Longing for something harder and thicker.

Dan gripped her hips and pressed against her rear, nudging at her entrance. First with his finger, testing her slickness by slipping in and out. When satisfied, he pinched her clit, rolling it between his thumb and forefinger until she clenched her fists on the sheets. A low whimper came from beneath her.

'Don't you dare touch your cock,' she whispered. 'You can't come yet.'

Sith began to pant. Sweat glistened on his heaving chest while his arms trembled. 'Ma'am . . .'

'You wanted me to tease you, make you beg over and over until every moment was an agony of waiting. I'm going to teach you never to ask for things you don't really want, Sith.' Her own breathing quickened as Dan added a second finger. She shoved back against him, still watching Sith. You're going to beg me to come tonight. In fact, I won't let you come until you beg. Lots.'

Lust and gratitude shone in his eyes. 'Thank you, Ma'am.'

'Watch me now, Sith. Watch *our* Master fuck me right in front of you.'

As though planned, Dan chose that moment to sink into her, heaving back on her hips to pull her on to him. For a split second Karen's toes left the floor, then she landed and braced herself against his powerful, pleasurable thrusts. No slow appetiser. No gentle warm up. Dan took her hard and fast, his hands never once leaving her hips. He leaned over her back and the curls of his chest hair scratched her spine, yet another sensation to add to the growing catalogue.

'It's like you read my mind,' he rasped into her ear. 'What better way to set the hierarchy than this? To make him watch and not touch. You, Karen, really are a Bitch Queen.'

Her laughter trailed off into moans as he licked her nape, her ear. Dan bit the side of her throat, not hard, but enough to make her squeal and shudder. The delicious pain of it cut across her breathing, reducing her to low, shallow gasps.

Something grazed her nipples.

Karen shrieked and looked down. Sith sat slouched, his head tilted back to catch her swaying breasts in his mouth. His hands remained linked behind his head, though his shoulders and elbows trembled with the effort to keep them there.

'Don't,' she began.

Sith's teeth closed on her nipple.

Pain stabbed through her, instantly melting into pleasure as Dan's rough thrusting morphed the bite into something else. Before she could recover, Sith bit the other nipple, leaving the first to tighten into a solid nub of hot flesh begging for more harsh treatment.

'Sith?' Dan's voice was rough with exertion.

Sith kept her nipple between his teeth. 'Yes, Sir?'

'Whatever you did to her, do it again. She tensed so hard I felt it all the way through me. Keep doing it.'

Karen had just time to see Sith's lips curve into a smile. 'Yes, Sir.'

He bit her again.

It took every scrap of will power she possessed to keep her hands on the bed. To keep her knees and spine locked. The assault on her nipples switched from biting, to licking, then back again. Sometimes he would lick one before the other, other times he would bite both, back and forth before switching to licking. The erratic pattern left her gasping and shuddering, fighting to predict what might follow.

Dan spoke again. 'Sith, make her come.' His voice cracked but the tone was strong.

'My fucking pleasure, Sir.'

Karen had just the presence of mind to snatch another dental damn from the pile on the sheets. She tossed it to Sith who needed no further encouragement. He ripped the packet open, spread the latex over her clit and set to work.

The sensation of a warm, quick tongue flicking her most sensitive button dragged shrill, senseless whimpers from her lips. She wanted to speak, to give orders, but Dan's incessant ponding, coupled with Sith's probing tongue made speech impossible.

Dan gave a shocked little cry. 'Fuck! I can feel your tongue, Sith. That's . . . good.' Shock and desperation tangled together in Dan's voice.

Karen's eyes flashed open as she heard her master call another man's name.

So hot . . .

Like every wet, sticky fantasy of her most wild dreams rolled into the real world and made flesh. It left her shaking, clenching, thrashing, moaning, darting out over the precipice of control and tumbling into bliss.

Stars of gold and purple danced before her eyes and she froze as the orgasm rolled over her, wave after mind-flattening wave of ecstasy until right was left and up was down.

Dan continued to drive into her, his pleasure building to a peak on the back of hers. His hands left her hips in favour of her shoulders, deepening his penetration. 'Kaz,' he breathed. 'Oh, God, Kaz, yes.'

Beneath her, Sith lay flat on his back, his hands bunched into fists near the waistband of those lacy red knickers.

'Please,' he cried. 'Please, let me come. Dear Christ, please, Ma'am, let me come.'

The ebbing pleasure rushed back in, cresting and breaking as she whispered, 'Yes, Sith. Come now.'

Sith sagged with relief, then instantly tensed again, grabbing his cock through the sopping wet lace and jerking once, twice, three times. He barely needed the last two. His orgasm ripped a groan from his throat, so raw and deep Karen feared he might hurt himself.

She saw his seed flood her stretched, useless thong and closed her eyes, painting the image on the fabric of her memory to enjoy for days to come. She released a slow breath. Unfurled her fists. Every part of her body still trembled and sang with pleasure. Her knees wobbled.

Dan withdrew. Though he did so gently, Karen yelped, sliding to her knees like a broken puppet. She landed beside Sith who was curled into a tight ball, hands tucked between his thighs. He seemed to be having trouble breathing.

She touched his shoulder. 'You okay?'

When he shifted to look at her, Karen understood for the first time what Dan saw every time they played. Burning lust. Pleasure. Satisfaction. Contentment. Exhaustion.

'I'm fine,' he murmured. 'What about you?'

'I'm great.'

Dan crouched beside them. 'Don't get too comfortable down there.' His voice was equally soft, but his dark eyes glimmered with mischief. He tossed his head to flick a curl of salt'n'pepper hair from his eyes. 'You still have work to do.'

He pointed at his slick, glistening cock, still hard and ready for action. 'You up to it, Kaz?'

She smiled. 'Always. Sith come hold me while I play with Master.'

Though weary, though weak, though clearly ready to curl up and sleep, Sith scrabbled up and sat on the floor. He spread his legs and Karen sat between them, the wet length of his softening cock pressed against her arse.

When she wiggled against him, he curled one hand over her thigh to gently tease her clit. The other hand returned to pinching her nipples.

'Ready when you are, Ma'am.' He whispered in her ear, husky and breathless, nibbling her earlobe after each word.

Dan gripped his shaft and directed the tip at her face.

Karen grinned. Opened her mouth . . .

*I hope you enjoyed that. ^_^*
Please . . . read on.

HELLOOOOOO SMEXXY READERS
Raven here! ^_^

Just wanted to say thank you for reading 'Second Base' second in my Slippers & Chains series. Hope you enjoyed yourself!

Since you're here, may I ask if you'd be willing to leave a review on Amazon and/or Goodreads? It doesn't have to be an essay – in fact it shouldn't! – just a line or two on whether or not you liked the story and if you'd recommend it.

I'm an indie publisher and reviews from folk like you help me reach the readers *umming* and *aaahing* over whether or not they want to join the party.

If you liked reading this book, chances are, they might too!

Cheers!

Raven Shadowhawk

ALSO BY RAVEN SHADOWHAWK

Slippers & Chains: Sugar Dust
Dan loves submissive women and longs to build a harem of willing females to fill what he lovingly calls his 'Slave Library.' He shares his plans for sexual bliss with Karen, the first of his submissives in his mind and his heart. But when an unexpected visit from his mother leads to uncomfortable questions about his ex, Dan realizes that past mistakes are catching up to him, faster than he can run.

The first D/s relationship to blend comfortably with her vanilla life is the one Karen shares with Dan. She treasures the freedom in the act of submission and wants nothing more than to share it with her Master for as long as possible. Why then, does he insist on bringing other women into their bed? And why can't he say he loves her?

As Dan battles his inner demons, Karen hopes a sexy mini break at the exclusive fetish club, Sugar Dust will allow them time to relax and reconnect. There she meets Beth, personification of Dan's past storming in to demolish her present. Can she show Dan that their relationship is strong enough to break the chains of his past, before Beth drives an immoveable wedge between them with her tales of what once was?

ALSO BY RAVEN SHADOWHAWK

The Meeting Each Other Series: The Full Story
When Vicki broke up with Malcolm she felt sure her life was over. She knew she would never find another love like the one they shared and her alcohol fuelled birthday party is but one of her coping mechanisms. That night, as she prepares for bed, unexpected company in the form of her best friend Lara, changes everything for her . . . and for the lives of many of her guests.

For the first time, enjoy the full story. Six different couples enjoy their first or most significant sexual encounters with their loved ones. This sizzling collection includes all six stories in the Meeting Each Other series and, for the first time, a secret look into how it all began in a brand new, wholly exclusive story told through the eyes of Lara Joyce.

COMING SOON FROM RAVEN SHADOWHAWK

Slippers & Chains: Picking Out Curtains

Slippers & Chains: Happy Families

Smexxy Snippets: In The Stationary Cupboard

Smexxy Snippets: The Backseat Of My Sister's Car

ABOUT RAVEN SHADOWHAWK

Raven ShadowHawk is one face of the author who writes fantasy and horror under a second pseudonym. She is, according to most . . . okay, according to *herself*, the fun one of the pair.

Living in Leicester, UK with her partner (the Funk Master) and twin sons (known as Sprog1 and Sprog2), Raven writes erotica ranging from sensual and romantic to graphic and totally PWP.

Her interests include badly produced porn, chocolate, dressing up (particularly in matching underwear) and shouting at women who wear stupid shoes and/or skinny jeans.

Newsletter: http://eepurl.com/oyKNj
Blog: www.ileandraXraven.co.uk
Twitter: @ileandraXraven
Facebook: www.facebook.com/illyandraven

www.ingramcontent.com/pod-product-compliance
Lightning Source LLC
Chambersburg PA
CBHW021044130626
46552CB00005B/2001